LEAVINGS

P .D. Cacek

LEAVINGS

P .D. Cacek

StarsEnd Creations

LEAVINGS

For information address: StarsEnd Creations
8547 East Arapahoe Rd. #J224, Greenwood Village, Colorado 80112

PRINTING HISTORY
First Edition, 1998
ISBN: 1-889120-10-3

Library of Congress Catalog Card Number 97-68713

Cover Art by David Martin
Published by
StarsEnd Creations
8547 East Arapahoe Road, #J224
Greenwood Village, Colorado 80112

Printed and bound in the United States of America
10 9 8 7 6 5 4 3 2 1

TO TOMI LEWIS

Contents

FOREWORD: BELIEVINGS

The 13 stories in *Leavings* do not represent the best the author can accomplish.

Now hold on—don't get that lynch-fever look. I hate that expression on the face of a literate, discerning, tasteful reader such as yourself.

I am not insulting the author variously known as P. D. Cacek, Patricia D. Cacek, or just plain Trish. What I am doing is embarking on a short explanation of one of professional writing's essential truths—that what you see in print is not representative of the status or progress of the author's present artistic evolution. What you read in print is a time-machine peek backwards into history. It's what the writer was creating months or years ago. She's somewhere else now—or at least she is if she's any kind of ambitiously worthwhile writer. And Trish Cacek is that sort of practitioner of the craft.

Actually it gets a great deal more complicated.

Good, effective writers don't improve at a steady arithmetical progression. The process is more of a quantum level leap forward/step backward sort of dance. To paraphrase an old maxim, a writer's reach should always exceed her grasp. On one hand, a writer such as Trish Cacek is always attempting to consolidate her gains and to build on the foundation composed of her past and present work as she each day carves out her future writing.

But here's what happens—I'm truly convinced—with a genuine wild talent. There are occasional times when a writer creates something she has no obvious right to achieve at this point in her career. She writes over her own head—sometimes successfully, many times not. Then, like an unexpected tidal wave, she subsides to her previous level and keeps on cranking out more of what one might expect for the time and level of ability. But those strange leaps forward are both exciting and daunting. The writer will eventually catch up to that level of achievement, will incorporate it into her mundane, every-day level of expertise. And then she'll jump ahead again.

Cacek did that precise thing with a short story called "Metalica" which appeared in Jeff Gelb and Michael Garrett's anthology, *Hot Blood: Fear the Fever*. Her tale of sexual horror is a wholly original tour de force which, alas, does not appear in this collection. "Metalica", a mere week ago as I write this, won the Horror Writers Association's handsome and respected Bram Stoker Award for achievement in the short story category for 1996.

That is a fine accomplishment particularly for a relatively new writer who has not published a novel. Cranking out novel-length work is not the required credential for becoming a recognized and respected writer. It's a respectable and respected art form, just as are poetry, essay-writing, writing for the screen or stage—and creating short fiction. In our little corner of arts and letters, I'd name-drop Harlan Ellison, Ray Bradbury, Nina Kiriki Hoffman, and R.A. Lafferty, to name but a few who established firm reputations as short-form writers before tinkering with novels.

I know that Trish Cacek has written novels and is working on more. I'm sure that when they appear, those novels will be accomplishments of the first degree. But for right now, it's the short story that defines her published writing.

She's good; no question about that. As you follow the story trail she's blazed in the pages of *Leavings*, you'll discover I'm right. If you are the sort of reader who demands unreasonable consistency in each literary outing, you may be disappointed here. Caveat lector. A worthwhile story collection assembles works of different textures, paces, tones. The baker's dozen within range from shocking to wistful. Straightforward icons of the shadowed horror genre occasionally appear. But more frequently, the author plays the angles, carefully planning unexpected carom shots that will take the reader unawares.

The title story is reminiscent, at least in tone, of such modern writers as Nina Kiriki Hoffman, or such classic storytellers as Zenna Henderson. This is a rural fantasy of wild talents, family inheritance (not always for the better), and especially, of relationships. That's the hallmark of just about all Cacek's fiction. Horror or suspense, sf or fantasy, the impact always generates from that most critical of story values—how human (and sometimes not-so-human) beings relate to themselves, to one another, and to the natural universe they inhabit. This is the preserve of the real writer, and Cacek's passport is valid.

In stories such as "Gilgamesh Recidivus" and "Yrena", Trish's characters visit the land of her ancestors—Russia, though the landscape is informed with atypical unicorns and perverse vampires, as well as the Russian Army and a bitter Leningrad winter. An unusual Merlin confronts a shrink in "Here There Be Dragons", while "Heart of Stone" mixes callous guys and gargoyles. A teddy bear you'd definitely want on your side stalks the generations of "Ancient One", and hard-edged wish-fulfillment fantasy grimly informs "Mime Games".

And so it goes. There are stories here of terror and love, courage and loss, obsession and letting go. When you finally reach the end of the collection, "Just a Little Bug" will pluck the strings of your heart like a blues guitar.

Is every story as successful as its fellows? Hey, these aren't link sausages. This is not corporate fiction. You may laugh, you might cry, but you're not reading these in lock step with every other reader. Each person picking up this volume is entering into a willing individual contract with the writer.

Be assured that she will hold up her end of the bargain.

So settle back, trust the author, and enjoy these forays into the dark fantastic. Then contemplate, with pleasure and anticipation, how more accomplished a storyteller Trish Cacek must now be, even as you read these words from her past.

Believe it.

—Edward Bryant
July 1, 1997
Denver

INTRODUCTION

"All we need now is for you to write an introduction."

Piece of cake.

I thought.

I mean, I'd already done the really *hard* part—I wrote the stories you're about to read. I created whole worlds and peopled them with (hopefully) realistic characters.

So how hard could writing an introduction to those worlds be?

Exceedingly hard, let me tell you.

When I write fiction, I know there's a kind of subliminal safety net that separates "me" from the characters and situations I create. It *is* fiction, after all and even though "I, the Writer" am in there...somewhere...I like to think I'm well camouflaged.

Well, I *like* to think it, but writing an introduction to those situations and characters changes the whole thing.

Now it's just me, *sans* costume and safety net.

Oy. But let's have a go at it, shall we?

Hi. I'm P. D. Cacek. Nice to meet you. Here, pull up a chair and I'll tell you a little bit about myself.

The first and title story of this book, "Leavings" took me almost thirty years to write. Now, hold on a minute...I ain't *that* slow of a writer, it's just that the idea took that long to gel.

From the time I first became aware of death (I mean *real* death, not the kind that happens to your goldfish) I wondered, as most children do, I'm sure, just what happens to all the "stuff" that made that person who and what they were: The smiles, the jokes, the way they had of moving or talking or telling a story.

It just didn't seem fair that "all that" got buried in the ground or, as we are told to ease our then still-fragile psyches, sent up to float around a cloud somewhere.

I figured there had to be more...something left behind of that person—even though I didn't have the slightest clue as to what that something might be.

Until my grandmother died.

Now, I wasn't a kid when this happened. I was in my twenties and co-teaching a class on Outdoor Wilderness Survival Skills; and to be honest, had given only the occasional, perfunctory thought to my childish preconceptions about death.

I was upset about her death, naturally, probably still brooding about it while leading a group of hikers through the Anza-Borrego desert. Okay, I was brooding a *lot* about it and missed the turnoff to the *only* source of water within ten miles.

Bad mistake. Major boo-boo.

And I wasn't worried for a moment.

Once I realized what I'd done, about twenty minutes later, I cut east and, picking my way carefully around the "jumping cholla" cactus and sun-bleached steer skull (a nice touch, I thought), led my little troop of city-dwellers directly to the water.

How?

I smelled it.

Now that doesn't sound too *Twilight Zone*, naturally...even though the wind was at our backs, even though I hadn't looked at a map in hours, even though in the middle of a desert summer water would be hard to smell in a canteen, let alone fifty feet below ground level.

Then how, you ask again.

Smelling water was something my grandmother could do. She called it her water sense and, up until that moment, it was something I had never been able to do.

Think what you will, but I think, *feel*, that this was a part of my grandmother, a very personal legacy that she left behind.

A "leaving".

The stories that follow in this volume all have that in common: That "something" is always left behind, passed on. Sometimes for the better, sometimes not.

So sit back and relax. Put your feet up, we're friends now. And maybe, just maybe...we'll leave something for each other.

—P. D. Cacek
Arvada, CO
May, 1997

LEAVINGS

The tarnished, mismatched spoon-chimes one of the grandbabies made—although now she couldn't remember which one or how long ago it'd been—hung in their protective place beneath the porch roof, silent and heavy in the still afternoon air.

Silent. Silence.

Agatha Mulvaney leaned back into the summer warm cushions and set the porch swing into motion with the balls of her feet. There was still so much to do, so much to get ready—but here she sat on the porch, under the self-same roof as the chimes and did none of it. Silent and idle as an almost bride on the morning of her wedding.

Idle. She liked that word. "Idle," she said softly and smiled at the flavor it left behind on her tongue: salty-sweet like the first dip snatched finger fast from an ice-cream churn. "Idle," she repeated a second time and let her feet continue to rock the swing slowly back and forth, back and forth.

That had been her Grammy's Leaving to her—not the idleness to which she had momentarily succumbed, but the tasting of words.

She remembered the day so well, the day words took flavor. The day her Grammy died.

Agatha's momma, who'd come from the City and only knew City ways, wasn't happy about being in the same house where someone lay dying (especially the bitter-tongued old woman who never let a visit end without making reference to "uppity city-bred folk"). Not happy at all. And let Agatha's daddy know it. Loud and often—her City voice ringing through the otherwise quiet house like the echoing chimes from the old mantle clock.

Years later and decades past, and all from that day gone to dust but her, Agatha was still glad her Grammy hadn't decided to die until after her momma had quit her fussing. The thought of what those words must have tasted like could still make Agatha's belly quiver.

Her Grammy had died just before sunset, Leaving Agatha's gift in the taste of honey and sassafras that suddenly filled her mouth when the old woman looked up and whispered good-bye.

It was only afterwards, after the sheet was pulled up over her Grammy's face and the others gathered round the deathbed all talking at once—her momma and daddy, neighbors and friends, the Preacher Man and relatives never seen before that morning—that Agatha got scared.

Thought the jumbled tastes of woodsmoke and honey and sassafras and tar that filled and faded and refilled her mouth were because she'd eaten one too many plates of some Cousin-somebody's pickled watermelon rinds.

And was afraid that any moment she was going to sick up all over her Grammy's body.

It took her a while, all summer and well into autumn, before she finally figured it out…before she finally was able to taste the words people spoke to her without gagging.

After that she got to like the flavors.

Most times.

And, even then, her Grammy's Leaving served her well (once she realized that neither her momma nor daddy were too keen about being told that their words said one thing and tasted another). She knew false friends the minute they spoke her name, could always tell what kind of hand her daddy was holding in pinochle by the taste of his banter on her tongue (green grass for a good hand, stale coffee if he was bluffing), and never tumbled for any boy's honey-sounding words that smacked of vinegar underneath.

Except once.

Lyle's words had tasted of cloves. Always tasted of cloves—strong and pungent and overpowering—hiding their true meaning; the cloying taste filling her mouth and leaving her…leaving…

Agatha dropped her heels to the porch, stopping the swing in mid-creak, and shook her head. She felt the skin around her eyes fold in on itself. Whatever relative, friend or stranger had left Lyle the gift to cloud minds and hide the taste of his words…she hoped he (had to be a he, she'd decided years ago) was still writhing in the agonies of Hell.

Forever and ever.

"Amen," she said out loud and smacked her lips.

Smiling up a whole different set of folds and creases, Agatha closed her eyes (idle old thing) and pulled in a deep, long breath of the late afternoon air.

Rain was coming. She could smell it—still far off, high over the broken-topped hills and wood lots to the west, but heading her way. That Leaving had come to her from the first boy she ever kissed back when she was only thirteen. He'd told her he always knew when it was going to rain because he could smell it. She hadn't believed him until the day he slipped off the fence line he was walking to impress her and snapped his neck. And the musty, cool scent of the approaching storm filled her head.

So many gifts.So many Leavings.

What would she Leave behind? Her green thumb? The way her joints ached when the wheat was ready to harvest? Or how it was that she always knew, without measuring, just how much salt to put into the gingerbread? So many things.

The scent of rain and summer hay and the whitewash she'd used on the porch not a month before mingled with the taste of grief whispering through the open parlor windows. Her grown children were talking about their daddy, their words heavy with woodsmoke and lye soap.

Lyle would have appreciated it, if he'd known how much they really cared about him. If he wasn't so busy dying.

A shout—high pitched and angry. And a taste that made Agatha grimace. Tar.

Opening her eyes, sorry that the idleness was at an end, Agatha stood up and walked slowly to the porch railing. The stiffness in her joints conjured up the memory of Lyle's braying voice—'That's what you get for bein' lazy, old woman.'—but, fortunately, not the taste.

The grandbabies were down by the duck pond—the six girls (three dark, those were Marjorie's; Celia's two pale sticks; and Tabby's chubby tomboy) gleefully tormenting Andrew, the youngest and only boy. It was his shout Agatha heard. His anger she tasted. Only nine and already so much anger.

So much anger. Just like his Grandpa.

The thought brought a taste to the back of Agatha's throat that had nothing to do with words.

Lifting first one hand, then the other, she fiddled with a wisp of hair that had come undone from the bun at the back of her neck. Keeping her hands busy always helped take her mind off unpleasant things.

"Now there, you children," she called out over the porch railing and down the long summer-dry lawn to the sniggering girls and red-faced little boy. "Stop your teasin' and fussin', hear? You don't get t'gether like this near enough to act like cats and dogs."

The girls looked up and smiled honey-gold radiance. Andrew pouted and kicked at a clump of mud by the water's edge.

"But he started it Grammy Mul," one of the dark-haired little magpies chirped.

The words tasted like salt.

"Now stop your fibbin' or else come inside the lot o' you. Hear me?"

"Okay, Grammy Mulvaney," the taller of the golden sisters called back. Waving. Her words, sweet cream.

"Okay," another added. Peppermint candy.

Andrew kicked the mud clod into the pond. And said nothing.

"Did you hear me, Andrew?" Agatha called again.

"Yeah," he answered sullenly, still looking down. "Okay."

Tar.

Agatha winced, smacking her lips as if that could somehow dispel the taste. It couldn't, well she knew, but she still couldn't stop herself from trying.

"Kids giving you trouble?" a low rumbling voice suddenly asked. Agatha turned and smiled up at her only son. "I can go have a talk with them, if they are. Maybe remind them of why they're here."

Yams and brown sugar and woodsmoke at the end. Agatha wrinkled her nose at the last flavor.

"They're fine, Martin," she said. "Let them be."

Looking at him was like looking into a Fun House mirror that showed things the way they'd been fifty-eight years before. Back when Lyle was a strapping young man, with the devil in his coal black eyes and courtin' in his coal black heart.

Maybe she hadn't known what he was like back then because he hardly ever spoke—just grunted and nodded like some old Tamworth boar. Grunts that tasted like cloves and shifted clouds around to the back of her eyes.

Grunts that took the place of words.

Their first baby, a boy, had come exactly nine months after that first rough, grunting tussle up in the loft of her daddy's barn…exactly nine months, but said to be a month "early" as a way to still the wagging tongues in town who had already started counting backwards to their hurriedly arranged wedding.

Not that it mattered.

The baby hadn't lived long enough to mew his first/last sound. Agatha never even got so much as a taste to remember him by. Nothing. Nothing to show that he'd ever existed except for a tiny white grave marker that read "Baby Boy Mulvaney/March 3, 1938" and the tiny white scar just below her left eye, lost now in a landscape of wrinkles, where Lyle had hit her—angry that he'd had to marry her for no reason after all.

She could still taste the words he'd hurled at her as she lay, still weak from childbirth and shock. Vinegar and wormwood and alum that puckered up her innards until she couldn't taste anything for almost a year.

Not that he said much in all that time. Just grunted now and again and filled the emptiness in her belly with Marjorie.

Agatha shivered remembering how she had actually begun to miss the taste of cloves and quickly rubbed calloused palms against her bare arms.

"You okay, Ma? Can I get you something? Why

don't you sit down and rest, you're…You shouldn't wear yourself out like this."

Golden peaches on her tongue. Concern.

Agatha lapped it up and shuffled over to him. Raised both hands and patted the firm muscles under his shirt. So like his daddy yet so little.

"Hush, now, I'm fine. Haven't been doin' nothin' but sittin' in that old swing almost all mornin'. Bein' lazy."

Martin's head was weaving back and forth like a blue jay looking for worms as he moved away from her and walked to the porch railing. He kept his back to her, pretended to be watching the children, but Agatha could still taste the woodsmoke when he spoke.

"Look, Ma, me and the girls were talking and, well, we thought it'd …. We thought it'd be nice if you came and stayed with one of us after Daddy's… After all this."

Agatha stuffed her hands into the apron's pockets and found enough lint and forgotten tissue to keep her fingers busy.

"This was my daddy's house even before it was your daddy's, and I'm comfortable with it."

"But, Ma…"

"We'll talk more on this later, Martin," she said, tasting the tar in her own words. "Right now I have to see how he's doing."

Agatha got as far as the front door when she heard "Feels like we're in for a storm" and looked back to see him rubbing the bristling hair on his arms. Where she could smell the rain, he could feel the lightning. That Leaving had come from a boy Martin saw blown into a thousand pieces in a jungle called Vietnam.

"Think maybe you're right," she said, then pulled the screen door open and stepped inside. "Best keep an eye on my grandbabies. I don't want them catchin' sniffles."

"Okay, Ma."

Agatha studied her son's broad back through the pinpricks of wire mesh—What Leaving would Lyle give his only son? And what, in turn, would he Leave his?—before crossing the entry hall toward the stifling, word-filled parlor.

Contrasting flavors assaulted her. Woodsmoke and tar; lemons and licorice. Some grief, some anger…but a good deal more greed and conniving hidden behind the sodden handkerchiefs and tear-swollen eyes.

Agatha paused in the doorway and looked in. Her daughters. Now that their baby brother had left the room, their true natures were pouring out of their mouths.

Marjorie, Celia, and Tabby (never Tabitha Rachel, as she'd been christened) were huddled together on the couch like plump and sniffling nesting hens. All so seemingly filled with remorse. All so eager to divide up the house and belongings that weren't even theirs.

Yet.

Agatha ahemed and smiled as each face, one by one by one, turned towards her. Only Celia, her middle-aged middle daughter, had the good grace to look like she'd just been caught with her hand in the cookie jar.

"How you doing, Ma?" Marjorie asked. Lemons and licorice.

"Holding up. How about you girls?"

Their three heads nodded as if "yes" was the correct answer to the question she'd just asked.

"That's fine," Agatha said, glad they hadn't said anything as she turned and shuffled toward the stairs. They started up again, tiny tastes of lemons and spice and everything nice, when she got to the first landing.

Another three steps, just past the squeaky one that Lyle had promised to fix for thirty-odd years but had somehow never gotten around to, and she tasted over-ripe pears.

Fear.

Agatha stopped and steadied herself against the banister, pressed her tongue up against the roof of her mouth and held it there. She'd tasted fear throughout her life. Many times and from many sources…but it still bothered her to taste it in Lyle's words.

Forcibly dragging her tongue back down where it belonged, Agatha snuffed loudly out through her nose.

"Aggie? That you?"

Pears, rotting on the stem.

"Aggie?"

Whining. Like a baby. Like a frightened little boy left alone in the dark. If she hadn't been afraid of what her own words would have tasted like, Agatha would have scolded him for that—dying or not—the same way he used to scold the children, Martin especially, when they called out in the night.

But she was afraid. Afraid that she'd like the flavor and use it like salt to season up a stew. Or rub in a wound.

"That you, old woman?" Pears blended with tar.

He was feeling better.

"It's me, Lyle," Agatha said as she pulled herself up the last few steps and across the narrow landing to the room they'd shared for almost six decades. "How you feelin'?"

It was a stupid question and they both knew it. Knew it even before the cancer born in his belly had spread to his lungs and consigned him to the old brass bed Agatha didn't even bother trying to polish anymore. Knew it.

But she kept asking.

And he kept answering.

"Tolerable." Woodsmoke with the pears this time. Almost palatable.

Almost.

Agatha smacked her lips as she crossed the room,

forgetting for the millionth upon millionth time how much he hated it when she did that.

"Will you stop the infernal suckin' noise, old woman, you ain't no nursin' calf."

Tar. He was angry. And Agatha smiled.

"Sorry, Lyle," she said. Brushing a wrinkle from the thick comforter that made her sweat by just looking at it, Agatha hefted the mattress gently and tucked the sheets in tighter over his legs. "You 'bout ready for the children?"

He looked up at her from his fortress of blankets and goosedown, skin tight over the bones of his face and yellow as a Buttercup. She watched the wrinkles ebb and flow around his mouth as he struggled to form the words.

"Just about," he answered. "Little ones, too?"

The bed springs creaked under their combined weight when Agatha sat down. It'd been a while since they shared the bed and she'd forgotten how pained a sound it was. Agatha slept in Martin's old room across the hall, peacefully on Cowboy-and-Indian sheets that still smelled of bubble gum and toothpaste.

"I think the girls are old enough to understand," she said, "But Andrew's still a bit young and ..."

"And you been fillin' their heads with that damned Leaving crap, haven't you?" He tried to grunt but started coughing instead.

Agatha pulled one of the wrinkled, more lint than substance tissues from her pocket and dabbed it against the blood-flecked drool on Lyle's lower lip.

He knocked her hand away once he could wheeze on his own.

"Damn foolish thing to believe in," he growled, tar dripping from every syllable. "That a person leaves something behind when he dies."

There was movement under the covers, but whether

he was trying to roll his shoulders the way he always did when he got mad or about to pitch another coughing fit, Agatha had no way of telling. Just to be on the safe side, she reached out and patted the flat, blanket covered plane below his chin.

He jiggled her hand away.

"The Good Lord show you mercy for your ignorance, old woman…the dead don't leave nothing behind but what gets put in the ground."

Agatha didn't argue. Didn't say a word. Just folded the bloodied tissue into her hands and listened to him sputter and mutter and remember, the flavors piling one atop of another until he drifted back to sleep. She made sure he was still breathing before tossing the tissue into the basket next to the bed and stood up.

Twilight had finally come and brought his breezy ladyfriend with him. The night wind entered the room through the open window next to the bed with a swirl of white starched curtain and the musty scent of rain. From below Agatha could hear the spoon-chimes tinkling like icicles.

Holding her breath, she stared down at the dying man's face. Lyle hated the chimes, always had, and only allowed her to keep them at all because she'd put them so high up under the porch eaves that they hardly ever caught the breeze.

If he heard them now…

But he slept on. Muttering. Words without meaning—tasting of honey. It wouldn't be long now. It always amazed Agatha that so many people were afraid of death when it was really so sweet.

A thin voice shouted from outside. A second and third answered.

Agatha added her own breeze to the room as she

hurried to the window. Martin had left the children to their games, even though the storm had covered the sky with its own thick blanket.

Bending low, and instantly feeling the strain along her back, Agatha poked her head out the window and waved.

"You children come on inside," she hissed at them—hoping she was loud enough to be heard over the rising wind, but not loud enough to wake her dying man. "Rain'll be here any time now and I don't want you catchin' cold."

The all encompassing "Aw" tasted like hot buttered corn, but they came running…Andrew lagging behind just far enough so his tattle-tale girl cousins wouldn't see him stop, look up at the house and stick out his tongue.

Agatha saw, was supposed to see, and stuck her tongue out right back at him. He giggled and ran after the girls.

"Little imp," Agatha said without thinking, then hurriedly crossed herself and kissed the knuckles of her hand; glancing fearfully at the bed as if the Devil and all His Legions were already snuggling up next to Lyle.

"Lord bless him," she added quickly, just to make sure, and just as quickly left the room.

"I'll bring them on up," she said when she got to the door, not so much for her man, who was still asleep, but for any Infernal Being who might have taken her slip of the tongue as an invitation. "And the Bible."

Lyle muttered—honey and tar—and opened his eyes.

"You know I loved you, old woman," he said. "You know that, don't you?"

Stale coffee. "I know, old man," she answered, shutting the door between them, "I know."

She didn't say another word until she was all the

way down the stairs. The grandbabies were in the parlor with their parents, chattering away about the pond and the approaching storm. Ignoring the shushes and hissed commands to "be quiet." Being children.

Agatha let herself taste the words a moment longer—green grass and woodsmoke, sweet corn and molasses, vinegar and apples—before going into the room.

The silence that greeted her was tasteless.

"Martin? Girls? You best go to your daddy now. I'll send the young ones up in a minute."

Martin looked like he was about to say something, then shook his head and led the way up the stairs. His sisters followed his example and, except for the occasional juicy sob into a fluttering handkerchief, said nothing in the way of comfort or condolence to her or themselves.

Thank God.

Agatha heard the bedroom door open and managed to count all the way to seven before she heard it close again.

"Is Grandpa really gonna die?" one of the little girls whispered, the words like slices of candied pears on Agatha's tongue.

She glanced from one play-flushed face to the next, trying to find the frightened whisperer. But couldn't. They all looked frightened. Except Andrew.

While his cousins clustered together in front of her like chicks caught under the shadow of a hawk, he was down on his knees, dusty jean-clad rump in the air, back turned to them; repeatedly ramming one of the tiny, impossibly detailed toy cars he'd brought from home against the claw-foot chess table Lyle's daddy had given to them before he died.

Along with Lyle's sudden love of the game.

It made Agatha smile remembering that.

"Your Grandpa is getting ready to leave this

world," Agatha said as if each child (save Andrew) had asked the question, "but it's not a sad time. Dyin's just part of life and your Grandpa had himself a very good life…full of all sorts of things and blessed with each one of you. Leaving it won't be hard."

She opened her arms and hugged as many warm bodies as filled her grasp. Only Andrew (naturally) and Tabby's chubby tomboy remained outside the circle of comfort. The tomboy sniffed loudly and tugged at the hem of a fancy, frilly dress that had to have looked better on the store's hanger than it did on her.

Andrew banged his car against the table. A white pawn fell.

"You girls go on up now and say good-bye to your grandpa…no, no—" What was the tomboy's name? Something absurdly feminine. Oh yes. "—Fiona, don't cry. There's nothing to cry about. Leaving is like a gift, the last gift a person can give to another. Now, you all go on up."

"What about Andy?" the youngest magpie asked as her sisters and cousins began climbing the stairs. "Isn't he gonna say g'bye to Grandpa?"

Agatha smiled and patted the child along. There were grass stains down one side of her cotton jumper. Marjorie would have a fit.

"He'll be up directly," Agatha said, shooing the child on. "Don't worry."

This time she got to fifteen before the bedroom door clicked shut. Andrew was still on the floor, rump still in the air, back still turned toward her. Still ramming his car into the table leg, the only sound a thin, metallic thunk.

"Andrew?" Agatha said, soft and easy—spun sugar candy—as she walked deeper into the parlor. "Andrew."

thunk thunk

"Andrew, the girls went upstairs to say good-bye to Grandpa. He's gettin' ready to leave us."

thunk

"Nothin' to be sad or scared about."

thunk THUNK-THUNK

"You're not sad, are you?"

The little boy lifted one shoulder. thunk

"Not scared?"

"No!" Pears. thunk thunk thunk THUNK thunk

"Didn't think so." Agatha looked down at him—straight back, arm moving back and forth (thunk thunk thunk) like a piston—and nudged him with her foot. "Let's you and me go for a little walk. How's that?"

He turned and looked at her, the very image of Martin at that age—soft green eyes and raggedly brown hair that wouldn't stay combed no matter what.

"You said we hadda come in 'cause it was gonna rain."

The taste of pears covered with tar. thunk thunk

"Well, it still is," she answered, hand stretched out—floating in the gathering darkness between her and her grandson like an insignificant cloud, "but I think there still may be a little time left. Besides, I'd love a walk with my only son's only son. Won't you do that for your old grammy?"

Andrew's rump remained the highest point as he turned back to his toy, head jerking once in what might have been a nod...or a silent gesture for her to leave him alone with his truck and the table leg. Agatha took it as the latter and bent down, using the tips of her fingers to swat his backside to the carpet.

He turned and glared at her.

So much like his grandpa.

"I don't wanna go for a stupid walk," he growled,

bottom lip protruding in what her daddy used to call a Rooster's perch. "Don't wanna."

Tar and vinegar tickled the back of Agatha's tongue. She had to swallow two, three times before she dared open her mouth.

"Well now, that's just too bad," she said, hands at her waist and foot stamping—hoping she looked every inch the picture of the mean old lady he probably already thought her to be, "because you're goin'. Now stand up before I call your daddy down here and show him what you've done to my good table."

The universal childhood fear of Dad, although Agatha had never seen Martin use more than a strong word with the boy, got him moving.

Slowly. Head down. The Rooster perch quivering. But moving nonetheless.

"I didn't hurt it," he mumbled, fingering the toy and Agatha smiled at the sudden taste of sour apples. Remorse. "You gonna tell my dad?"

"Well, I don't know ..." she said and tipped her head sideways just enough to make it look like she was examining the table. In truth, she could barely make out where the piece of furniture ended and the carpet began, let alone see the leg in question. But she hemmed and hawed a moment longer—just for good measure—before straightening up and winking at the boy.

"Guess there doesn't seem to be any more damage than what your daddy's shoes already put there back when he was young. Now about that walk ..."

The minute old threat still seemed to be working. Andrew instantly came to her side like a well trained puppy and, if not a little begrudgingly, even took her hand until they got to the gravel walk out in front of the house. A quarter of the way down the path leading to the out buildings and the taste of sweet grass and peppermint candy filled his words and Agatha's mouth as he began to chatter on and on about the wonders of toy cars and video games and basketball and this "...really cute girl in class with blue eyes and yellow hair, except she's kinda stuck up and only plays with other girls and doesn't look at me even when I make mouse noises."

To demonstrate, Andrew, the toy car momentarily forgotten in the throes of puppy-love, pressed two fingers firmly against his lips and sucked air in around them.

The resulting high pitched squeal did sound like a mouse. One that had been caught in a trap.

"My, my," Agatha said, hand coming to her swaying bosom to show how impressed she was, "and this little girl doesn't find that wondrous?"

"Nah." Andrew stooped, picked up a rock and threw it into the trees lining the path. Agatha heard it strike its mark—a dull hollow sound that was followed almost immediately by the low rumble of thunder.

She looked to the purple tinted west and sniffed the air.

The rain was close, Martin's lightning dancing in the clouds. Exhaling the damp smell from her lungs slowly, Agatha looked back over her shoulder. The house hidden by the trees, but she knew if she stared long and hard enough she might be able to make out the line of the porch or the peaked, slate-gray roof...or even the upstairs bedroom.

How much longer would it be, she wondered.

"—uck up, do you, Grammy?"

Agatha blinked and turned around. Andrew was looking up at her, an ernest, serious look pinching his face.

"I'm sorry, honey, what did you say?"

The seriousness darkened, mirroring the sky. "I said, that she shouldn't be going around bein' so stuck up all the time."

Noticing that her hand was still at her chest, Agatha fumbled with the rolled edge at the top of her apron and frowned.

"Who shouldn't, honey?"

The storm broke—both on land and in the air.

"You weren't listening! I was telling you about this stupid girl bein' so stuck up and you weren't listening! I hate you, I hate you! I wish you'd die like Grandpa! I wish you were already dead!"

He took off running, the soles of his shoes kicking up the rain splattered dust in clumps as Agatha hurried to catch up, but falling farther and farther behind—the wind snatching away the words almost before they left her mouth.

"Andrew! Come back here. Andrew. Stop running and come here to your Grammy. Andrew. I'm sorry I wasn't listening. Andrew. Don't go inside. Andrew!"

The heavy summer rain became a liquid shroud long before Agatha got back to the house, covering her completely. On the porch the swing twisted on its creaking chains and the spoon-chimes clashed like swords. The sound echoed down along the eaves and crashed against Agatha's eardrums.

She barely noticed it. Barely noticed the wild hammering of her heart as she looked through the sheeting rain for the boy.

But Andrew wasn't on the porch or in his daddy's car (which he had refused to leave when they first arrived); nor was he standing next to the door, shamefaced for having yelled at his grammy and scuffing out the toe of his shoe.

He wasn't anywhere Agatha looked. The only other place would be the house…but she didn't think he'd be that foolish to run in all wet and out of breath to face his Daddy's imagined wrath at having left his poor old Grammy out in the storm.

At least she prayed he wouldn't be that foolish.

"Andrew?" she called again as she pulled herself up the last step and felt the solid porch beneath her feet. "Andrew, it's okay, Grammy's not mad at y—"

And then she heard it, tasted it—like cool cider on a sweltering day. Weeping. Lyle was gone. Lyle had Left.

Agatha took a deep breath of the rain rich air and nodded. Thank God.

"Oh, Grammy," Fiona, the tomboy in lace, whimpered as she rushed out of the dark house and into Agatha's dripping arms, "Grandpa's d-d-d—yuck, you're all wet!"

Agatha hugged the child to her, shivering from the delicious warmth against her belly.

"Hush, now, hush," she said, soothing back the boyishly short hair, "it's all right. Grandpa's in a better place now. I'll betcha he's up in the sky with the Lord already…smilin' down on us right now."

The chubby little girl looked doubtful and snuffed up a double noseful of tears.

"You sure, Grammy?"

Agatha hugged her tight. "Sure'n anything, baby girl."

"Okay," she answered, rubbing the top of her head against the underside of Agatha's breasts. "I guess. Don't be sad. I'm sorry I…"

Without finishing what she was going to say, the little girl reached up and touched the side of Agatha's face, her stubby little fingers tracing the cheekbone down to the chin and beneath. Chucked it once.

It was a small thing, almost forgotten. That had been Lyle's way of apologizing—a gentle touch instead of having to mouth words that might fumble on his tongue. It had been the one thing she used most often as a balance when his sins tipped the scales inside her.

A gentle touch. His Leaving to their poor, misnamed grandbaby.

If Agatha had ever loved him before, not that it mattered anymore if she had or not, she loved him now and would mourn his passing.

"You run back inside," she said, feeling the chill left on her skin when the child moved her hand away, "I'll be along directly."

Fiona, the tomboy, disappeared into the dark house without a second glance.

From where she was standing Agatha couldn't tell if Andrew was inside or not. Where was that little…She huffed and started across the porch. Pretty soon she'd have to stop worrying about the boy and start thinking about turning on lights and getting the supper ready.

Almost as if by thinking it she'd commanded it to happen, Agatha saw first the parlor and then the hall lights blink on. She tried not to smile but couldn't help herself. Lyle had left somebody (and she only prayed it was one of her grown children) his fear of the dusk…not the dark. Lyle was too much a man to be afraid of the dark, but the dusk made him jittery.

The porch light went on.

"Ma! What are you doing out…oh, my God, you're soaking wet! What happened? Were you out in the rain? What were you doing out in the rain? Don't you know you could catch your death of cold? Oh, my God, I'm sorry I said that—I wasn't thinking, I —"

Lyle used to jabber on like that while he fought the dusk.

"Oh for Heaven's sake, Tabby," she said, walking into the house and ignoring the barrage of questions that still came at her, "we don't need all these lights!"

Tabby followed her almost to the stairs before making a quick detour to turn on the dining and alcove lights.

Poor Tabby...and poor Tabby's husband when he got their next month's light bill.

Agatha was about to say something to that effect when Martin suddenly exploded from the parlor like a runaway freight train. "Oh. Ma. I wondered where you were. You're all wet." His voice was flat, husky with emotion, tasting of burning cottonwood. "Um, Pa's ..."

"Fiona told me." Agatha smiled without trying to. "You and the girls okay?"

"Yeah. Fine." He cleared his throat. Scuffed one shoe against the other. Flexed his hands—open, shut, open. "Excuse me a second, Ma."

Tar flavored his words, coating Agatha's tongue as she watched him slam open the screen door and march—purposely, straight backed—to the far end of the porch and snatch the spoon-chimes from their decades old home.

"These were driving me absolutely nuts," he growled at her through the screen mesh. Smirking as he tossed the rusted spoons into the howling night and wiped his hands off on his pants before coming back inside. "I don't know how you could stand them all these years. Want me to get you a towel, Ma?"

Agatha nodded...thought she nodded...must have nodded because she watched him bound up the stairs to the bathroom. But she wasn't sure, because she was busy remembering. None of the grandbabies had made the chimes. Martin had. Back when he was no older than his son. Made them from the discarded spoons he'd found in the "junk" drawer because he said he loved her so much.

Lyle had cuffed him hard on the ears when he heard that, then smirked when the boy screamed in pain. The smirk had looked identical to the one that had been on Martin's face not a moment earlier...when he'd thrown his chimes into the storm.

Her Grammy never said a Leaving could be directed to someone specific. And Agatha had never thought to ask.

Until now. But now was too late.

Agatha shivered as she walked to the parlor, the towel Martin had given her before disappearing back into the storm clutched in her hand.

One of Marjorie's dark daughters was curled up on the couch, looking out the window, shoulders knitting silent sobs. Her sisters were less affected. They, Fiona and one of their blond cousins, were jostling each other for position in front of the portable television Martin must have brought down from the bedroom. The second blond girl was wandering around the room. Straightening. Smoothing out a fold in the curtains, palming straight the rows of books in the shelves, making tiny adjustments to the china figurines on the mantle. Touching. Fingering. Wiping. Sorting.

Just like Lyle used to do during a storm.

Andrew wasn't in the parlor. Or the dining room. Or the kitchen. Or anywhere on the first floor that Agatha's slippers left behind wet footprints.

She was coming back to the entrance way when the upstairs hall light snapped on.

Tabby stood at the top of the stairs—hand pressed against the light switch, teeth scraping the pale peach color off her bottom lip.

"It's just so dark in here, Ma."

Pears—overripe and putrid.

"That'd be the storm," Agatha said, already more than halfway up the stairs, the damp towel fluttering over one shoulder. "Why don't you go on down and fix yourself a cup of tea…or something."

Both of them knew that the something was the bottle of Rye whiskey Lyle had always kept in the pantry for "medicinal purposes". Agatha hoped he hadn't Left his need for the "medicine" along with his fear of dusk.

"Yeah, maybe...that sounds like a good—" Tabby started down a half-dozen times, one foot then the other inching toward the first step only to be pulled back a moment later, before sighing and glancing back over her shoulder at the closed bedroom door. "I mean, it's just so...strange to think of him...gone. You know what I mean, Ma?"

Agatha knew. It was like a cold, windswept mountain you're used to seeing all your life suddenly not being there one morning. Agatha knew.

"Go downstairs," she said, then waited until her daughter did so before asking, "Have you seen Andrew? I think the lightning frightened him."

"Oh," Tabby said, more calm now that night had finally swallowed dusk, "he's upstairs with Pa."

Agatha said one word, "ah", then didn't say another until she opened the bedroom door.

"Andrew?"

The boy looked up at the sound of his name and smiled. He was standing next to the bed, one small hand resting on top of the covered body of his grandpa. Tabby had turned on every light in the room, including the painted clam shell nightlight Agatha had bought for twenty-five cents at the last Church Bazaar. The brightness made Agatha squint. It didn't seem to bother Andrew in the least.

"Hi, Grammy."

Green grass and peppermint candy. And soft gray gathering around the corners of the too-bright room.

Agatha moved slowly to the opposite side of the bed and lay her hand over his. His skin was warm, only a few rain tears glistening in his raggedy, uncombed hair.

"You been up here long, Andrew?" she asked,

squeezing his hand just a little, just enough to let him know she forgave his temper tantrum and hateful words.

"Not too long," he answered. The smile on his lips faded when he looked down at the covered form under their hands. "Grandpa's dead."

"I know, honey. Were you here when he ...?"

Andrew looked up and blinked, his brow furrowing deep wrinkles.

"When he what, Grammy?"

Agatha sighed and moved closer.

"Were you here when your grandpa died, baby," she said, soft and gentle so not to frighten him, "or did you come in after?"

The little boy's grin returned, as bright as any of the lights his poor jangled aunt had turned on.

"Oh! After, Grammy," he said.

And the taste of cloves filled Agatha's mouth.

"I'm sorry I ran away," Andrew pouted. "I guess I just got kinda mad n' stuff, 'cause you weren't listening just like that stuck up ol' girl in class. But I really don't wish you were dead...honest. I love you.

"You won't tell my daddy, will you?"

The room was filled with clouds—soft gray clouds that made everything look so much nicer. Agatha smiled.

"You won't will you, Grammy?" her grandbaby asked again. Her sweet little boy.

"No," she promised, squeezing his hand, "of course I won't."

BABY DOLLS

They looked too damned real.

Maybe that was why he hated them.

Each eyelash had been curled and placed by hand. One at a time. Individually. Painstakingly. Lovingly.

(costly)

And so damned real looking it made his skin crawl.

That was the thing Ben Willowbranch couldn't understand. Why would anyone want a solid porcelain baby doll that looked so real? He remembered how his kid sister wouldn't sleep in the same room as her bug-eyed (bug-eyed since their dad had backed over it with the station wagon) Betsy-Wetsy doll because she said it looked too real.

Not that it had, even before its unfortunate accident with the snow tires; but if that had been his screwy sister's reaction to a molded piece of plastic, then he had to wonder what a doll that looked like a real sleeping baby would do to a normal child's psyche.

Maybe instead of a framed affidavit insuring that each lash on their baby dolls had been placed individually, LUV-a-Bye, the company manufacturing the dolls, should offer coupons good for future psychotherapy sessions. One per customer.

Redeemable on demand.

Good idea, Ben thought, but one that would probably bankrupt the company in a year.

No parent in their right mind would buy their kid a doll that cost almost four times as much as he made in a month.

Maybe.

Although, since becoming a "Sales Associate" (salesman) at Porcelain Angels (eighteen months ago) to augment (sustain) his real (non-paying) job as an up and coming (middle-aged crisis) commercial artist, Ben hadn't noticed many right minds walk into the store. Little old ladies with blue hair and fixed incomes, harried husbands being dragged from one doll to the next until it was time to pull out the ol' MasterCard, teenage girls plunking down half of their minimum wage earnings each week on porcelain princesses, cigar-scented businessmen smirking for investments, Baby-boomers buying memories...but not a right mind as far as Ben could tell.

Some people, he always mentally added after the transactions and thank you's, please come again's were completed, had more money than they knew what to do with.

He, of course, wasn't one of them.

And, unless he got a substantial raise in the near future or some rich relative he'd never heard about suddenly dropped dead and left everything to him, would never be one.

Once, when he was draping fake ivy into what he hoped would eventually look like a wooded glade for the "Bambi and Family Miniature Collectibles", Ben calculated how long it would take for him to pay off the most expensive piece, The Great Prince of the Forest...should he accidentally drop it.

The answer shocked him. Badly.

Even with his twenty percent employee discount (and ignoring for the moment, since this was fantasy, all the real bills that had to be paid each month), he figured it would still take him over a year to pay off the five by seven inch, "Real Bone China" buck.

And Bambi's dad was a mere piker in price compared to the doll Ben was dusting at the moment.

The too-damned-real baby doll. The kind he hated.

The thought made him look down, which was a bad mistake. He had intentionally (and, up until that moment, successfully) avoided direct visual contact since lifting it from the pale blue (since "it" was a "boy") LUV-a-Bye display box.

Really, really bad mistake. Even though he was supposed to be dusting it.

Frowning, Ben brushed the soft, multi-colored feather duster across the red porcelain curls and heard the scratch of material against ceramic. His stomach quivered at the sound, then tightened with envy…the way it always did…when he allowed himself to marvel at the artistry that had created the doll.

Maybe that's why he hated them so much— because he knew he could never do anything as realistic…as breathtakingly beautiful as that.

Ever.

Ben stopped the duster just under the point of the second, chubby fold of chin and leaned closer. The newest addition to "The Nursery", No-Name Boy #5786-B (LUV-a-Bye, Inc., preferred to leave the naming up to the "Adoptive Parents") had a ruddy red face and slight frown. A tiny pout played across the extended lower lip; and the hands, each one curled into fists, were tucked in close, protectively across to the front of the blue LUV-a-Bye and Goodnight sleeper.

The doll didn't look happy. In fact, "he" looked down right pissed off.

He was, Ben had decided almost immediately (after

the shock of seeing him buried beneath mounds of shipping peanuts and shrink wrap wore off), his favorite.

If he had a favorite.

Which he really didn't.

Because he hated them.

Every last one of the overpriced, individually lashed, nationally originated, racially correct, real looking dolls.

Especially this one.

This one that reminded him so much of Miriam. When she was pissed off.

That made him think what their child might have looked like.

Had she let it live.

Ben stood up too quickly and knocked a small, hand-printed sign off the top of the display bassinet. It landed right side up, it's gold-edge black lettering crisp and clear:

> Please do not pick up our babies.
> They're sleeping and do not
> want to be disturbed.
> —Thank you.

Ben's hand was shaking a little when he replaced the card. Right, he thought, so much more pleasant than saying "You break it, you bought it."

He saw Miriam again in the tiny porcelain frown as he stood. She'd frowned just like when he told her how much he really wanted to be a father.

"How's it going, Ben?" a voice suddenly called. It took him a minute to recognize it as M'Lynn's, the store's owner, calling from the main showroom. "Are the babies all behaving themselves?"

Ben managed a smile as she swirled through the

thin gauze curtain that separated the "Nursery" from the rest of the store. He guessed her to be somewhere around his own mid-forties in age, although in reality she could be a decade on either side. Trying to determine a woman's age, especially a beautiful woman had never been Ben's forte. And M'Lynn was beautiful…tall and willowy with thick coffee-colored hair that fell just below her shoulders and eyes the color of summer grass.

Today she was wearing a pale green dress that deepened the faint rose color of her cheeks and complimented her eyes.

A tiny porcelain fairy in matching green leaves ($19.95 plus tax) dangled from a golden chain just above the hollow of her throat.

"Oh, just fine, M'Lynn," he said when he was finally able to drag his eyes back up to hers. "Except this little one. He doesn't seem too happy to be here."

M'Lynn's entire demeanor changed. It was fascinating, like watching a quick moving storm overtake a bright summer's day.

"Oh, dear," she cooed to it, "whatever could be wrong?"

Ben crossed his arms over his chest as he stepped back to give her room, hiding his growing smile behind the dust cloth. He couldn't fault her business sense—Christ knew where she found people willing to spend thousands of dollars on what was nothing more than painted chunks of expensive clay—but her devotion to the dolls, especially the baby dolls, bordered on the fanatic.

And that was sad, because without that one flaw he might have fallen in love with her.

Deeply in love.

Ben felt the smile disappear and let his arms drop back to his side.

"Poor little thing," M'Lynn said as she traced the curves and waves of the porcelain hair. "He does look sad, doesn't he?"

It, Ben wanted to remind her, not he...It.

"Maybe he knows he's on sale."

M'Lynn's eyes flashed when she looked up—green lightning—an instant before she noticed he was joking and laughed; dimples that more than rivaled the crafter's art adding exclamation points to her cheeks.

"Oh, you."

"No, I mean it," Ben said, keeping the joke going because it kept her there, less than an arms length away...separated by only the wicker bassinet and its frowning (price reduced) tenant. "Being a bargain's pretty hard on a guy, especially when he's new in town. I know." Ben let his shoulders slump. "I've been there."

M'Lynn leaned back on one heel, cocking her head to one side. The porcelain fairy danced at the end of its golden tether.

"Oh, so you're a bargain?"

Ben nodded, reshaping his face to match the doll's. Pouting.

"Absolutely. With a twenty percent discount for employees."

Her laughter washed over Ben's chest and shoulders and lifted the hair at the back of his neck as it passed. Maybe he could love her, fanatic obsession with dolls notwithstanding.

"You know," she said and ruined the whole thing, "you really would have made a wonderful father. It's such a shame you didn't have any."

Ben nodded and pretended it was a compliment. M'Lynn knew about his divorce and lack of offspring; his hopes of becoming a "real" artist and lack of faith on ever achieving that goal…that had come out during their first lunch together, more by chance, just something to talk about rather than through direct questioning…but he still pretended. And kept quiet.

Just like he always did.

Just like he always had.

Keeping quiet when Miriam had told him she wanted a career instead of children; and counted the reasons off on her fingers: They were expensive, required almost constant care until they were old enough to go to school, and were an emotional drain.

Keeping quiet. Pretending he understood. And agreed.

No. No children. Not now. Not ever.

Ever came eight weeks after their fifteenth wedding anniversary—an accident brought on by one too many strawberry Margaritas and a substantial raise (hers naturally, he'd been "downsized" back to the Unemployment Department a month earlier).

She was frowning when she told him, the frown hardening when Ben did the unthinkable…and stopped being quiet.

They could afford it, he'd said.

They'd love it.

They'd protect it from harm.

He said. He bargained. He pleaded.

He begged.

And got drunk while she was at the clinic having the tiny dab of inconvenient flesh scraped and flushed from her body.

He was still getting drunk a week later when Miriam told him she wanted a divorce. She'd just got rid of one baby, she told him, and she wasn't about to let him try to take it's place.

When she hadn't returned to the apartment by midnight, Ben half-stumbled into the bathroom and vomited; after which he cleaned out the tub and himself with a series of HOT-hot/COLD-cold showers until he felt capable of half-stumbling on with the rest of his life.

Two years and three states later and he was still half-stumbling; although now he was Gulliver half-stumbling through a porcelain Lilliput.

God, if Miriam could only see him now…surrounded by baby dolls to replace the child they never had.

"Is there something wrong, Ben?" M'Lynn asked.

He gave her the first lie he could think of. "No."

"Sure?"

"Sure."

"Good, because I need you to help me set up the display for the Cat in the Hat commemorative plates and miniature tea sets. You're so artistic I don't know how I managed without you."

He never should have told her he was an artist.

Ben considered altering the first lie into one that described a headache the proportions of which might well indicate a brain hemorrhage. The last thing he wanted to do was fumble around with maniacally grinning cat plates and tea cups no bigger than the tip of his little finger, both of which would cost more than an arm and leg if he broke them.

No, take that back. The last thing he wanted to do was to continue dusting the porcelain baby dolls.

Smiling, Ben tucked the duster under one arm and dragged the tip of one shoe across the variegated blue-gray-pink carpet.

"Aw, shuckens, ma'am. Yer gonna make me blush."

M'Lynn reached over the bassinet and squeezed Ben's arm lightly before she turned, laughing, and glided back through the gauze curtains. The motion was captured and echoed in the antique cheval glass mirror she had him place in one corner of the room, so the "adopting parents" could see themselves with their new "babies". Silken vines of pink and blue Morning Glories cascaded down along the beveled edges and another of the tiny porcelain fairies, its chain tether scotch-taped and hidden behind a curling leaf, hovered near the top of the glass.

It really was a magical effect.

Except for the reflection it sent back.

Ben waved and watched the man inside the glass— middle-aged and gaunt cheeked from years of eating things for their convenience instead of nutritional value, the K-Mart "Blue Light Specials" shirt and slacks hanging from the bony six foot frame, the hair too long and too gray, the eyes too dark and too hooded—wave back. The rainbow duster added just the right amount of color contrast.

And realism.

Self-Portrait of the Artist as a Loser.

By Benjamin Ray Willowbranch.

A bargain. Take two. Special twenty percent employee discount.

Ben shook his head and watched the man in the mirror copy him. He hated the man in the mirror even more than he hated the dolls. If that was possible.

"Okay, Ben," M'Lynn called, "whenever you're ready."

Her gentle way of telling him to get his ass in gear.

"Be right there," he said to the mirror, then turned—too quickly—and bumped the bassinet with his hip. The frowning doll that reminded him so much of Miriam shifted; one hard little knee bumping against the padded side.

#5786-B didn't look any happier with the sudden change, if anything it looked as if it really were about to cry.

God, he hated it.

Sighing, Ben stuffed the handle of the duster into his back pocket and scooped the doll up, one handed, intending to smooth the blanket and setting it down as quickly as possible.

He never got the chance.

M'Lynn burst through the curtains, a freckled-faced little girl and just-as-freckled mother in tow, while he was still holding it.

"See," M'Lynn whispered as if it really was a Nursery, and the frowning doll he was holding like a football really was only asleep, "didn't I tell you he was wonderful with babies?"

Both freckled faces looked up at him and smiled. The doll suddenly felt heavier then its listed inventory weight of 7 lbs. 10 oz.

"Now, Ben, these ladies are looking to adopt one of the babies, and since you're our expert ..."

He looked down at the doll. Since when was he an expert?

"... you can work on the display later," M'Lynn said, her voice still hushed, and slipped through the curtains like a pale green mist.

"Oooo," the smaller of the freckled-faced gushed, "he's frowning. Look, Mommy, he's frowning."

For a moment Ben wasn't sure who the little girl was referring to, him or the doll.

"What's his name?" and "How much is it?" came simultaneously. Ben reapplied his salesman's grin and carefully transferred the doll back to its bassinet, tactfully avoiding the small outstretched hands on the way down. The danger of letting the child hold the doll was obvious…at least until her mother bought it. Or one like it. Then he wouldn't care if the kid decided to kick it all the way home.

"He doesn't have a name yet, sweetheart," he told the little girl as he straightened, keeping one hand on the bassinet just in case she tried to make a grab for the frowning object of her momentary affection. "You get to name it— him when you adopt him."

To the mother he said, "The price is on the tag. Layaway requires thirty percent down and we can hold it up to a month," then pretended he didn't hear the sharp intake of breath when she actually saw the price.

"Oh. My. Ah, look Magda…look at all the other babies. You don't want to get your heart set on that one when there are so many others."

The ploy worked.

Squealing with delight, the little girl began flitting around the room, pointing to one doll after the other as the "one she really, really wanted." Ben stood aside and just watched. He didn't have the heart to tell the mother that she'd already seen and rejected the only sale item in the room.

He also didn't get around to the Cat in the Hat display until a half-hour before closing. And by then it was too late to do more than unpack and inventory each tiny piece and curse, silently, under his breath.

He'd also developed a headache, a real one that went far beyond the one he'd thought about making up earlier that day.

An apparently obvious one that M'Lynn treated with two aspirin and a can of Pepsi from the machine in the stock room.

"Thanks, boss," Ben said, dry swallowing the aspirin as he worked the pop-top open. One of the aspirin felt like it got stuck half way down his throat and even three long gulps of fizz wasn't enough to take the feeling away. "I needed that."

"I could tell," M'Lynn said as she tucked her skirt under her and sat down on the floor next to him. It was something she never did when there were customers in the store, so that meant they were alone. Except for the dolls. But he didn't think they'd mind.

"You really knocked yourself out today, Ben. How many babies did you find homes for? Two?" She'd picked up a sheet of bubble wrap and was snapping it, absently, as she spoke. "Three?"

Pop. Pop.

Ben smiled. M'Lynn never said sold...that would smack too much of reality, but he found it endearing. In a way.

Taking another sip, he nodded his head as carefully as he could (the aspirin hadn't kicked in yet) and shrugged one shoulder (also carefully).

After Mom and Child Freckles left, with the frowning baby boy, christened Billy, a half-dozen more "Prospective Parents" had been ushered into the nursery and left in Ben's care. Within the hour he had found homes for three dolls (Jumoke, Xiu Mei and Titania) and filled out Lay-away slips on five more.

"Just doin' my job, ma'am," he said, pleased that she'd noticed.

M'Lynn bumped his arm with her elbow, playfully. "No, it's more than that. I've had Associates before who were only doing their job, so I can tell the difference. You like what you do. You like the babies."

Pop. Pop.

Ben took another sip to keep his mouth busy. He'd already blown a marriage and chance at fatherhood by talking—he wasn't about to repeat that same crime now. Not if it might mean losing him another job...and possible love interest.

"They're beautifully done. The craftsmanship, I mean," he said. No lie that—they were. "I'm envious at the artist who could achieve such...er...uniqueness. No two dol— I mean babies are alike. Everyone of them is different. Just like real ones. Babies."

M'Lynn smiled and took his hand. Her fingers and palm were warm.

"Just like real babies," she whispered. Leaning closer she kissed him. Now he was sure they were alone. "Only our babies are loved right from the start. Loved and cherished and wanted...not like some real babies. Sometimes a real baby isn't wanted. Not wanted. Can you imagine such a thing?"

Ben tried to swallow. Couldn't. It felt as if the aspirin had somehow managed to inch its way back up his throat.

"Yeah," he nodded, "I know."

The pressure on his hand increased. "I knew you'd understand, Ben. I knew it from the moment you started working here...the gentle way you have with the babies."

She gave him another quick kiss and stood up, brushing the wrinkles off the back of her skirt with the protective wrap.

"Let me just lock up and I'll meet you in back. You can leave the display until morning, okay?"

Ben nodded, at least he thought he nodded. The aspirin had finally kicked in, with the help of the Pepsi's caffeine and sugar, but he still felt fuzzy and light-headed. Maybe he just needed to be kissed on a more or less regular basis.

Standing only made it worse. Walking helped, but not much.

She took the can from him at the door of the storage room and hugged him. He hugged back, kissing her cheek, mouth and neck before forcing himself to pull away. The porcelain fairy smiled up at him.

M'Lynn was frowning.

"There was a problem with this morning's shipment from LUV-a-Bye," she said, stepping back into the room and pulling him along. "One of the babies…was damaged."

Ben saw a tear form and fall, sliding down the curve of her cheek. He kissed it away quickly. Christ, no wonder she was upset. As with most of the manufacturers of overpriced collectibles, LUV-a-Bye, Inc. didn't have a return policy. Places like M'Lynn's had to buy the object first, full wholesale price; no questions asked, no quarter given. If it happened to arrive damaged or in pieces, tough.

Better luck next time unless you're real handy with Super-glue.

"Hey, it's okay. You've got insurance, right?" he asked, hoping he sounded concerned. "I mean, it's an awful loss, but …"

There was something in her eyes besides tears, something that told Ben he had chosen the wrong path and was in imminent danger of stepping off into a chasm from which he would never be extracted. He back-peddled quickly.

"I'm sorry, I know that probably sounded crass and unfeeling. It's just that …" Ben took a deep breath and tried to mold his aspirin dulled thoughts into something that sounded—plausible. When that didn't work, he went for pathetic.

"Well, these little…things are special to me, too. And, the thought of losing one is—" He shrugged. "I guess it's a guy thing, we don't like to show emotions so we pretend to be insensitive clods. Just like now."

It did sound pathetic. Worse, it sounded contrived.

And M'Lynn bought every contrived, pathetic syllable of it.

Whatever danger Ben saw in her eyes a moment earlier drowned beneath shining green waves. He swallowed a sigh of relief.

"You are so sweet," she murmured, rewarding the lie with another, longer kiss. It wasn't the first kiss Ben had ever connived from a woman, but it was the first time that it felt wrong.

When M'Lynn broke the embrace and took his hand, pulling him deeper into the storage room, Ben followed without hesitation. He owed her that much, he decided when they got to the faux-antique roll top that served as M'Lynn's office, maybe more.

A pink "LUV-a-Bye" shipping box lay across a scattering of pamphlets, flyers and catalogs on the desk pad; its top crushed, a red, white and blue UPS "Damaged in Transport" sticker just below the shipping label. Ben could just imagine what the doll inside looked like.

"I'm so sorry, M'Lynn." He knew she secretly preferred the girl baby dolls. He'd seen her in the Nursery when she thought he was busy with a customer, talking to the pink sleeper-clad toys as she cuddled them to her. It was sick, but maybe if she had a real baby of her own .... "What can I do to help?"

M'Lynn was crying in earnest when she finally looked up at him.

"They're usually so careful, Ben," she sniffed, hand reaching toward the box then moving away. Quickly. Clutching the fairy pendant as if to stop herself from trying to touch the box again. "You have to believe that. This is only the second time ..."

Her voice broke and Ben had the overpowering urge to clear his own. Instead he moved in close, pressing against her back and kissing the top of her head.

"M'Lynn, it's okay…really. It's—" He caught himself before "just a doll" tumbled out. "It's going to be okay. Do you want me to…throw it away for you?"

She spun away from him, hand still clutching the pendant as she moved behind one corner of the desk.

"M'Lynn? What's the matter? What did I say?"

Ben took a step toward her and her hand flinched. When she released pressure a tiny pink leg and part of a leaf-green wing fell to the floor. Shattered.

"Throw it away?" she repeated, eyes wide, tears poised like rain; heavy, waiting to fall. "Ben, throw it away? That's what her parents already did, Ben. They threw her away." A tear broke free. Fell into the shadows lining her mouth. "And we weren't there to catch her."

Ben took a deep breath and held it a moment before letting it go. All this fuss over a broken doll. The woman was nuts. Crazy. What a waste.

"M'Lynn."

"We have to bury her, Ben," the crazy woman sobbed, stepping around the desk to his side again. "We owe her that much."

It was odd hearing his own thoughts put into words…made his flesh bunch into goose bumps because now it was being used for some damned toy. But he nodded and pretended it was a reasonable request.

Like stringing fake ivy or setting up miniature tea parties. Or selling baby dolls that looked too real.

"Okay," he said and reached for the box.

M'Lynn stopped him before he could touch it.

"We can't bury her in that," she sighed, "not wrapped in plastic and packing peanuts. Wait." A smile, of sorts, came to her lips. "I'll use one of the quilted blankets we just got in."

Ben watched her go and shook his head. Fine. If she

wanted to wrap a broken doll in a hand quilted crib-blanket that retailed for $37.50 and then bury them both, fine. No skin off his nose, no pennies out of his pocket.

He'd all but decided to start checking the Classified in the morning when he sliced through the reinforced strapping tape and brushed a handful of packing peanuts to the desk top. He was still thinking about it, weighing the Pros and Cons of having to find another job, when he tore open the plastic sheet around the doll's face.

And jerked backwards.

Christ, not only was the doll damaged, but something must have spilled on it. It smelled rank!

Ben tried breathing through his mouth, until the smell became a phantom taste on his tongue. Frowning, he did the best he could with short, shallow breaths as he leaned forward to check the damage.

The head had suffered the worse of the damage; shards of peach colored porcelain spiderwebbed the left side of the tiny face. The eye on that side had been cracked up, the dark auburn lashes matted with some kind of thick, yellowish resin that puddled beneath the tiny, perfectly formed ear. That was where the smell originated, he decided after a longer whiff.

Like rotten meat...or something.

Ben nodded as he straightened. Whatever damage the good folks at UPS thought they did, it was obvious that the doll had been broken long before that. Probably at the factory. That would explain the foul resin drip...or whatever it was.

"M'Lynn," he called, grabbing the doll by one arm and lifting it from the box; the neck had been broken as well, it hung at an odd angle, almost dangling.... "I think you might be able to get your money back on thi—"

The head twisted away from Ben and a shard came

loose and fell, bouncing off the edge of the desk before dropping to the floor. Ben didn't notice where it went, or even if it shattered like the broken pieces of fairy, he was too busy staring at the space where the shard had been. He knew the dolls weren't hollow, they were too heavy for that; but he'd never expected this.

It had to be some new kind of plastic, he heard a voice inside his head explain calmly, or clay...some weird kind of mold they used before dipping them in the porcelain bath. Something...

... anything other than what it looked like.

Ben held his breath when he touched the patch of pale, almost colorless flesh the broken porcelain had uncovered. It was cold, the texture of old rubber; soft and giving, but lifeless, holding the impression of his fingertip; the tiny blue veins unchanged, undisturbed...empty.

He looked at the hardened resin covering the side of the tiny face and felt his stomach turn.

When he exhaled it came out sounding like a sob. He was cradling the broken baby against his chest when M'Lynn came back with the quilt.

"I know it's hard, Ben," she said, cajoling the baby from his arms, "but we have to bury her."

"B-but...but—" All he could do was point and watch M'Lynn wrap the dead baby in the quilt. "It was real! That was a real baby!"`

M'Lynn looked up. "Well, of course she was, Ben. All of LUV-a-Bye babies are real...were real until their parents got rid of them, threw them away like they were trash, like they didn't matter. They never had a chance when they were real and growing, Ben—but they do now."

Bending forward, M'Lynn kissed the broken little face before covering it.

"The people who would have bought her would

have wanted her, Ben. You've seen them, our customers. You've helped them…you know how much they want these babies. Want them, Ben. If this little one had lived," M'Lynn said, gently running her fingers over the quilt, "she might have been abused or tortured…because she was never wanted. She was a mistake…that's how her parents saw her…just a mistake to get rid of. But this way she would have been wanted and cared for. And loved. Forever and ever.

"You understand, don't you?"

Ben felt himself nod. It almost made sense. Unwanted babies suffered. Wanted dolls were cherished and dusted and cared for. He watched M'Lynn pick up the little porcelain corpse and hug it gently.

"I knew you would, Ben, you would have made a wonderful father. There's a place I know, a small grove of trees not too far from the children's playground by the lake. It's so pretty there." M'Lynn stopped looking at Ben. All her attention was now directed at the bundle in her arms. "Oh, yes it is, it's so pretty and there are lots of squirrels and bunnies and ducks to play with."

She was smiling, glowing when she finally remembered Ben was standing there.

"She won't be alone, Ben. She'll have a little brother to play with." M'Lynn tipped the bundle closer to her chest, cradling the head and neck as if it were still alive and breathing. Above her hand, the broken fairy smiled at him. "He, I named him Geoffrey after my father, was one of LUV-a-Bye's first babies. They didn't have the technique down as well as they do now and he was…well, he was in very bad shape when he arrived. I had to bury him all by myself, Ben, and that was so hard.

"I'm so glad you're here with me."

Ben nodded again. There was little else he could do. He'd been selling the dolls…the babies for how long?

His stomach did another tuck-and-roll and tried to crawl up his throat. He swallowed it back down.

"And I don't think we'll have to worry too much about this sort of thing happening again," M'Lynn said, picking up one of the flyers from the desk and handing it to him. "LUV-a-Bye is starting a brand new line and we've got the exclusive rights to sell them. Isn't that wonderful?"

M'Lynn beamed as Ben took the flyer and began reading. At first he didn't feel anything, as if he'd been the one dipped in porcelain, then his stomach fell through the soles of his shoes.

LUV-a-Bye PREEMIES:
The Tiniest Babies for the Biggest Hearts to Love

Ben looked back at M'Lynn as the weight of the paper pulled his hand down to his side.

Fetuses. Tiny unwanted dabs of flesh that had been scrapped and flushed away.

He wondered what the cost would be after his 20% employee discount.

"You want to drive?" he asked. "Or shall I?"

M'Lynn handed him the quilted bundle and kissed him. "I'll drive, I know the way. You can think of a name for her before we get there."

"Already have one," Ben said as he walked with her to the back exit. "Miriam."

MIME GAMES

Callie Beaumont was raped on her lunch hour—in broad daylight and in full view of witnesses—and every one of them applauded.

And threw money.

Callie's only thought, when she joined the other working class drones on the noon-hour exodus, was to put the world temporarily on hold and get lost in urban anonymity.

And the small municipal park across from the office complex in which she was entombed from seven-thirty in the morning to four-thirty in the afternoon (five days a week, fifty-one weeks out of the year) seemed like the ideal place to accomplish such a task.

Not much more than a greenbelt with benches, the park separated four of the worst lanes of congestion the city had; and offered little in the way of a challenge to the League of Corporate Joggers that roamed the city in packs.

The fact that Callie had never seen anyone in running togs do more than traverse the park on their way to indoor tracks (fully equipped with air-conditioning and digital lap counters) only added to its charm as far as she was concerned.

A small herd of nooners crossed with her, complaining about the late summer heat and the price of gas and how that new V.P. in purchasing only got the job because he was the boss's nephew, and continued on...still complaining.

Callie leaned against one of the minimally maintained shade trees and watched them go...thanking whatever metropolitan god happened to be in the area that they hadn't followed her into the park.

She could feel the tightness across her shoulders begin to ease as she turned. There were maybe a dozen people (if that) taking advantage of the park's smog drenched seclusion...all of whom seemed intent on ignoring each other.

Perfect.

Since most (if not all) of the shadier nooks were already occupied, Callie followed the meandering path to the park's central quad...a ten foot by fifteen foot rectangular slab of concrete which hosted a broken drinking fountain and three benches donated by a local chapter of the VFW.

Usually no one sat in the quad but her. Usually.

A middle-aged woman in a summer weight linen suit was sitting on the first bench, methodically peeling an egg. Dammit.

Veering toward the last bench, Callie glared at the woman and ...

...felt her shoe come down on someone's toe.

"OhexcusemeI'm ..." The automatic apology caught in her throat as she turned.

The mime was hopping around in circles in front of her, fanning the "injured" foot with a derby hat as he alternated between mouthing curses and shaking the hat at her. An instant later, he planted the foot and twisted his black leotard body into an old-fashioned fighting stance—derby tipped back, hands curled into knobby fists.

Put up yer dukes. The clown-white lips formed. Puttem up.

Callie shook her head and sidestepped him…or, at least tried to. He countered her every move, shifting from pugilist to waltz partner in a manner of seconds. An instant later, he cartwheeled into a handstand without missing a beat.

"Wonderful."

Callie turned and saw the woman from the front bench stand up and start applauding like a kid at her first circus; her so carefully peeled egg lay squashed on the cement at her feet.

"Bravo."

Acknowledging the praise, the mime pivoted on his hands and flexed his elbows in an inverted curtsy. When a quarter hit the cement a yard in front of him, he curtsied again.

Seeing her chance for a fast exit, Callie turned toward the trees at the far end of the park just as two more quarters sailed past her face.

"Really something, huh?" A businessman asked, as he and a construction worker bracketed her. "I always love watching these guys. Don't you?"

Callie glanced back at the mime instead of answering. Just my luck, she thought, I have to find the only street-performer aficionados in the whole city. The mime was still on his hands, lifting himself onto his fingertips as he pirouetted in a silent ballet. When a of couple one-dollar bills floated down to join the change, Callie took the hint and began fumbling with her purse.

Like a dog sensing a forthcoming treat, the mime scurried up to her and began bouncing up and down on his palms.

There was more applause, and more people appeared at the edge of her periphery, but Callie didn't look up. She could feel the blush start at the base of her throat and shoot through her cheeks as someone laughed.

Crumbling a five-dollar bill in her hand, Callie smiled and purposely threw it behind him. The mime darted to the left, faded back and—BOP—caught it between his knees.

Pop fly...yer out.

The applause was almost deafening.

The crowd of blue and white collars had somehow surrounded her while she wasn't looking, and Callie felt a chill replace the blush left on her skin. When the mime curled forward—feet overhead—and flipped into a standing position, then arched his back and shoulders in an Olympic dismount, Callie forced herself to join in the applause...all the while looking for the quickest way back to her office. Suddenly the idea of sitting behind her desk and listening to all the latest soap opera gossip sounded incredibly appealing.

The mime bowed to the crowd and the handfuls of coins that hit the concrete sounded like hailstones. (Good, it's over.)

Callie took a deep breath and started pushing her way through the crowd when someone spun her around...back toward the mime. Again there was the sound of laughter and coins falling to the ground.

The mime was standing directly in front of her, one hand fluttering against his chest—the standard routine—part of every mime's repertoire for showing immediate and undying love.

Standard. Routine. Like walking against the wind...or being trapped inside a glass box...(trapped)

Callie tried to muscle her way through the crowd, but the same pair of hands held her fast.

"Uh-huh, can't let you go just yet, sweetheart," a deep voice boomed in her ear. "Not after your boyfriend went and got you flowers."

There was nothing she could do but watch the mime pick imaginary flowers (daisies) out of the cracks in the sidewalk.

Circling his thumb and fingers to indicate a small bouquet, the mime cocked an imaginary hat into a rakish angle and offered them to her.

She refused.

The crowd supplied the sound effects as the mime visually crumpled. Broken-hearted. Dejected.

"Shit, I wouldn't put up with that from my woman."

Callie spun on her heels and glared at the man. He was wearing a sweat-stained Hard Rock Cafe tee shirt and biker's glasses...not the usual type to be seen hanging around the city's financial district during business hours.

"Yeah, cold man...arctic." This came from a Junior-Executive type in a three piece suit.

"I don't think we should judge her like that." Mrs. Egg-peeler said. "She's probably just shy. Maybe if he tried again ..."

"Naw. Lady's as cold as ice. I think he should ..."

"Maybe candy instead of flowers ..."

"Maybe a good swift kick."

Callie watched the mime silently entice suggestions from the crowd then act out each in turn. The suggestions, as well as his movements, becoming more violent...more suggestive. But only she seemed to notice.

Someone bumped her from behind, muttering "Bitch". Mumbled agreement from the crowd.

(This is getting crazy.)

"Look," she said, forcing a smile at the gyrating mime, (Jesus, what's he doing now...a whip...whipping someone? Oh, God.)

"This has been...a lot of fun. Really. B-But I've got

to get back to work." To make it as convincing as possible, Callie glanced down at her watch and frowned. "God, I'll be late if I don't ..."

She turned into the crowd...and they turned her back. Again. Toward him.

His face as expressionless as the painted mask it wore.

"Yo mama, you ain't going nowhere." Someone in the crowd answered for him.

"Not until you apologize." A different voice added.

"But I really have to go."

"As I've already stated, you're not going anywhere." This voice was different than either of the first two...but that didn't matter, Callie suddenly realized, because the faces and voices in the crowd were no longer acting as individuals...only parts of a whole.

Snapping open her purse, she withdrew two bills and without bothering to notice if they were ones or twenties, threw them at the mime. The money hit his chest and fell, unnoticed, to his feet.

He took a step closer, crushing one of the bills beneath a slippered heel, and cocked his head. Slowly, he lowered himself to one knee and held out a single (imaginary) flower (daisy).

(Be nice...just take the damn thing and smile. Be nice.)

Callie tried to clench her jaws to keep the words in but it was already too late.

"Get away from me!"

There wasn't so much as a whisper from the crowd as the mime slowly got to his feet. As he backed up he shook his head.

"And I thought you were something special." The teenage girl to Callie's left snarled.

"You people are crazy!" She finally screamed at them. "I'm going to find a policeman and ..."

She gasped and grabbed her chest as the crowd roared with laughter.

The mime was standing a yard...two yards away, fondling the air in front of him—his long fingers following the contours of her breasts. (This isn't happening. Can't be happening. I don't believe...)

He pinched the air and she yelped, her hand automatically covering the throbbing nipple.

"Stop it."

Her whisper was lost in the sudden applause. The mime was undoing an imaginary belt, unzipping an invisible fly...

"Yeh, c'mon man, do her."

"Teach this woman some manners."

The crowd was back...content for the moment just to sit and watch.

Callie screamed as his hands slashed through the air. She felt the skirt of her dress tear apart at the front seam. Dropping her purse she doubled over—tried to hold the pieces together—only to feel his hands on her shoulders...pushing her down to the hot cement...holding her there.

"Help me...please!"

The crowd chuckled.

His fingernails tore grooves down the inside of her thighs as he worked her panties off. An instant later he was on top of her, prying her legs apart with his knees.

A few men in the crowd whistled their approval.

Callie's back arched an inch off the ground as he tore into her. He laid down on top of her and his weight almost suffocated her. She opened her mouth to scream and found his lips clamped over hers. His tongue tasted like chalk.

Twisting her head to one side, Callie vomited as he came inside her.

The crowd cheered.

Another shower of coins pelted the concrete around her, but this time the sound was cushioned by the layer of bills that preceded them.

Callie pulled her legs into her belly and curled around them.

"Help. Me."

Polite applause. Nothing exceptional. The show was over.

"Jesus, look at the time."

Other voices carried the sentiment as individuals drifted back into the real world of summer heat, outrageous gas prices and VPs who were related to their boss.

A man wearing an IZOD shirt and $200.00 jeans grabbed Callie's arm and pulled her to her feet. When she moaned and tried to cover herself with her hands, he chuckled and winked at her.

"Great stuff. You guys ever do lodge meetings? I know a couple of places…"

Callie heard his voice rumble on and on like summer thunder as she stared down at herself. The front of her dress was wrinkled and smudged at the hem where she'd rubbed it against the concrete in the struggle, but other than that it was unmarked. Whole. Untouched.

The IZOD man finally got tired of trying to talk to her. Callie watched his shadow shrug then jaywalk against traffic to join the returning Lunch Hour Refugees. When she built up enough courage to look up, the Mime bowed deeply and swept the derby hat low across the scattered donations. A dozen bills tumbled over each other like leaves in the wind.

"You son-of-a-bitch. What did you do to me?"

Callie took a step forward and doubled over, barely

making it to a bench before the second cramp hit. Something gave way deep inside her and she groaned.

A shadow slid up her legs and into her lap.

"Get away from me."

A single daisy fell against her clenched fists as the shadow disappeared.

Callie was still staring at the flower when the evening rush swept through the park and carried her along with it.

***

She found him again in February.

Standing with arms outstretched, he was cavorting in front of a late afternoon crowd of business types who normally would have had better sense than to stand out in a misting rain.

Normally.

But there was nothing normal about it. If the Mime wanted a crowd, there'd be a crowd. If the mime wanted a woman…

Callie brushed the damp hair out of her eyes then jammed her hand back into the pocket of her black pea-coat. This time he was only going to get what he deserved.

Keeping her head down, she slipped into the crowd without anyone noticing. Not that anyone would have noticed. They were all too busy applauding the Mime's attempt at capturing the heart of a frightened teenage girl.

"Son of a bitch," Callie hissed, but no one heard it over the first faint rumblings.

"Geez, man…she's even colder than the weather."

"Hell, no woman of mine'd git 'way wid actin' so stuck up."

"Yeah. Show her who's boss."

Not this time, you bastard.

He was on his knees in front of the girl—one hand extended toward her, finger tips touching, the other beating a gentle tattoo against his chest—when Callie shouldered an old man aside and stepped out into the open quad.

For a moment, she was invisible—overpowered by the Mime's "performance"—and then someone saw her.

And laughed.

"Whoa there, good buddy…maybe you'd better be checkin' in with the Missus 'fore you try brandin' another filly."

The Mime turned toward her, pivoting on one knee, and Callie swept the ground in a deep bow. Despite the biting chill, the clown-white greasepaint on her face felt hot and sticky. She had drawn a giant tear-drop under one eye with blue eyeshadow and elongated the downward curve of her mouth in eyeliner.

The crowd loved it.

"Uh oh," someone snickered, "Mama don't look too happy."

The Mime stood and took a step toward her. As he did, the teenage girl bolted, muscling her way through the crowd.

And only Callie…and the Mime noticed.

He took another step and, one black slippered toe trying to work itself into the damp concrete, offered her the flower. (a daisy)

Not this time.

Pulling her hands from the coat, Callie marched up to him and knocked the offering from his hand.

"Oooo," a voice murmured, "you're gonna get it now, man."

"Yeah…shouldn't be playing around where the old lady can see you."

Callie raised one fist and shook it an inch away from his face. Building on the memories she had of her mother's tantrums, she stamped her feet and tore at her hair. Just for good measure.

The Mime backed up a half-dozen steps, circling to the left when the crowd refused to let him pass, and shook his head. Callie followed close behind, ranting in closed mouth silence.

"God, I'd never let my boyfriend get away with something like that."

"Men. They think they can get away with anything."

"You dog, you."

Callie let him get a dozen steps away, before reaching into her coat pocket and pulling out the gun. The crowd knew it was a gun because she made it out of her fingers—thumb raised, index finger extended and pointing straight at his heart.

"YEAH, do him lady...you don't need that shit from him."

"Pretty little thing like you having to put up with a bastard like that."

"Do it."

He knew it was coming and turned to run...but it wasn't any use. Callie took careful aim and fired twice, rocking back on her heels each time the silent, pantomimed recoil shuddered through her body.

"All right."

"Nailed that sucker good."

"He ain't gonna be messin' around with no other women, that's for sure."

The Mime lay on his belly, arms loose at his side, one leg twisted under the other: The perfect picture of a dead man.

Taking a deep breath, Callie carefully slipped the gun back inside her pocket and bowed.

The crowd was still applauding when she turned and walked away.

Callie was almost out of the park when she heard the first scream. Someone must have turned the Mime over—probably wondering why he was still laying there instead of entertaining them—and seen the gaping holes in his chest.

Smiling, Callie lifted her finger to her lips and gently blew over the top of it.

THE PRINCESS

"Once upon a time, so long ago
that I have quite forgotten the date,
there lived a king and queen who had
no children."

Veronica sighed and closed the tiny book, drawing her fingers slowly across the embossed leather cover that was already beginning to show signs of wear. Father had brought it back from one of his business trips down the coast. It had been wrapped in white tissue and tied with a red satin ribbon, and Veronica's heart had pounded with anticipation…until she saw what it was. *The Light Princess*, by George MacDonald.

A fairy tale.

"It came highly recommended by the clerk," Father had told her proudly, his great barrel of a chest puffing up to even greater dimensions beneath his gabardine waistcoat. "Apparently this MacDonald is quite a fine author when it comes to writing children's books. Please note the inscription on the front's piece."

To which Veronica had immediately turned and silently nodded her appreciation to the flowing script.

"To Veronica Marie Warren," it read, "the most obedient child a man might have. From your loving father, Carlisle Ambrose Warren. May 23, 1867."

Veronica sighed again and slipped the book into the pocket of her overskirt as she stood. Her father was kind and generous, with that she had no fault, but he stubbornly refused to see her as anything but a child. And she was already well past the mid-point of her twelfth year.

A fairy tale, indeed; and one that, had her father deigned to read it, told of a daughter who was most singularly not obedient. Veronica stamped one of her patent leather boots against the wooden porch and felt the book jiggle deep within the voluminous folds of her skirt.

A fairy tale! Veronica stamped her foot again. And such an incredulous one at that…all about a silly Princess who, because of a curse laid upon her at birth, was able to defy the law of gravity. Fantasy, pure and simple.

Father, being the scholar and amateur scientist that he was, would have made her burn the book had he found out its true nature.

Which was the reason Veronica was very glad he had never read it and why, despite her ire at its being childish and stupid, never mentioned the book other than to thank him whenever he found her curled up with it amid the pillows of the hotel's settee.

Veronica felt the blush rise to her cheeks, pushing away the chill of the afternoon's foggy gloom. It was such a fanciful little story…and yet she loved it so.

The blush worked its way down her cheeks and into the high starched collar of her blouse as she walked to the porch railing. The condensed beads of dew soaked instantly into Veronica's kid gloves when she absentmindedly ran her hands across the white-washed wood.

She "tsked" once but wasn't terribly concerned. Father wouldn't notice, besides which she still had the "good" pair of gloves, the ones that had been her mother's, wrapped in tissue upstairs in her room.

Waiting for her.

Waiting.

How long?

Removing the soiled gloves, Veronica tucked them into her unoccupied pocket and reached for the gold lapel watch Father had pinned to that very blouse the night before.

"To mark the hours until my return," he had told her gravely, her eyes narrowing as he fingered the tiny watch. "This was your mother's. I expect you to take care not to break it."

Telling her that. As if she were a child.

The blush in her cheeks and neck deepened into something far hotter.

Veronica was all ready to stamp her foot again when the sudden trilling call of a gull broke the silence. Gray and white, its wings arrow sharp, the bird swung upward into the sky before darting down again below the cliffs beneath the raised wooded train platform. A tiny shiver, so tiny that Veronica decided to blame it on the cold, tickled its way up her spine.

They had arrived at the hotel a fortnight ago at twilight, the fog already beginning to curl itself catlike around the sea-cliffs below the trestle. Just looking down as she'd disembarked the train…straight down into the narrow gap that separated track from platform, and seeing the crashing waves two hundred feet below had given Veronica such a queer feeling in the pit of her stomach that she had been unable to take even the lightest supper that evening.

But that had been when they first arrived. Now, whenever she wasn't reading or doing the lessons Father had set down for her, or when the dullness of the hotel became just too dreary to bear, she would walk the gravel path to the train platform and watch the waves endlessly pound at the cliffs with great blue-gray fists.

Forever.

How long?

Something clattered from inside the hotel, making her jump and driving the nagging question from her mind. Contradicting its title and main character, the tiny book felt like a stone in her pocket.

There wasn't any one at the hotel but her—the traveling salesman ('tis bound for Seattle, I am, don'cha know) and three maidenly school teachers with whom she and her father had shared the evening's meal had all departed…the salesman on the same morning train as Father and the teachers by hired carriage to visit, they had told her over tea and biscuits that morning, some of the quaint vineyards farther inland. Even the hotel's owner and his good wife had left despite their obvious reluctance to do so.

"This is our usual day to go into town for the marketing, miss. But I dislike leaving so…young a guest unattended. Would you care to come with us?"

The thought of going into the town only seen fleetingly from the train windows almost proved too much temptation. Veronica had not been a hundred yards off the hotel grounds since arriving. As per Father's instructions.

"I thank you for your kind offer," she had answered, "but my father told me to remain here and await his return, and that is what I shall do. As for the other, I am perfectly capable of taking care of myself." Then, seeing suspicion in the older woman's eyes, Veronica had raised her chin and crossed her fingers behind her back. "I have been left on my own a number of times since my mother's death three years ago. Do you believe me so young that I warrant constant supervision?"

Veronica didn't know what she would have done had the landlord and his wife answered "Yes" to that final question. It was true that her father occasionally needed to leave her alone in strange hotels while he occupied himself with business…but highly untrue that he ever allowed her to stay alone.

She being just a mere child.

Veronica had held her breath as she watched from the window of her room, shivering in the pre-dawn cold until her father was safely aboard the train. Father would only be going as far as Fort Bragg and only for the day…but it would still give her more than enough time to…

…time…

…to do…

"Whatever I please, I suppose," Veronica said out loud.

And a paper thin voice answered her.

But this time she didn't jump. She ignored it.

Because it was what one did with ghosts. Father said.

"There are no such things as ghosts, Veronica," Father had told her rather gruffly their first night at the hotel when she had awakened to the trembling sensation that something was in the darkened room with her. "But even if there were, you have the option of ignoring them. And you may trust me when I tell you that nothing on this plane or the next takes to being ignored for very long. Therefore, if you suspect you are being accosted by a spectral visitation, my suggestion to you is that you ignore it until it feels so ill used that it departs of its own free will.

"If such things existed."

The explanation might have been more acceptable, Veronica had decided silently, still trembling beneath the starched linen sheets and handmade quilt, had Father not swept into her room while dressed in a flowing white night-dress, his hair and beard disheveled, and the normal hollows of his usually placid features underlit by the single, flicker-ing candle he carried.

If Veronica had been the child he thought her to be, the consequences of his sudden appearance might have been disastrous.

"But I'm not a child," she reminded herself. "And there are no such things as ghosts. Father said."

So Veronica ignored the next sounds she heard from the supposedly empty building: that of a cup shattering and the murmuring laughter which followed.

"I'm ignoring you," she said and, fingers clutching her mother's watch, spun on her heels ...

...the scream tickling the back of her throat, before Veronica realized the pale, wide-eyed reflection staring back at her from the hotel's dining room window was her own.

Her breath, cradling the aborted scream, came out in a long, slow sigh.

"What would Father have said if he'd seen you?" she asked the dark haired girl in the glass. Then frowned. And watched her reflection do the same. Father would undoubtedly have said nothing, since he saw her only as a child.

Veronica took a step closer to the dark glass and turned to one side, the frown deepening.

Perhaps if she had been beautiful, like her mother, Father would have finally noticed how grown up she was becoming. But even as she indulged in a moment's impromptu preening Veronica knew it was hopeless.

She was as ugly as her late mother had been beautiful. Dark, where her mother had been fair...with Father's drab hazel eyes instead of the cornflower blue she had (as a child) prayed they would eventually lighten into. And thin...so dreadfully thin and flat where she remembered her mother's figure as seemingly forever discontent to remain within the confines of whalebone stays and tight laces.

Arching her back, Veronica took a deep breath and

tried to inflate her depressingly tiny bosoms. Nothing. Tried again until she thought her lungs would burst…again with no discernible effect. The heavy traveling cape and over-skirt, made even heavier (and uglier) by the fog's penetrating damp, clung to her like a woolen shroud—concealing all.

If only …

If only she had been born beautiful, or in some way reminiscent of her mother, Father might be content to spend more time with her. If only…

Without feeling her own hand move, Veronica watched her reflection's fingers slip into the overskirt's pocket.

…if only she were like the Light Princess who's disregard for gravity extended to a lightness of character which allowed her never to feel things too deeply…

Her reflection shimmered in the glass, lengthened, grew blond whiskers and spectacles. The ghost blinked at her, its mouth forming a startled "O" even as it faded.

An illusion, Father would say. A flaw in the glass. Just ignore it.

Veronica didn't realize she'd been holding her breath, waiting for the flaw (with its trimmed beard, wire-rimmed spectacles and curiously fashioned high neck shirt) to reappear, until her lungs felt ready to burst.

But only her image hovered in the glass.

Only her.

When she finally allowed herself to exhale, her breath exploded into the chilled air, mingling with the drifting tendrils of fog and disappearing. The whole experience left her feeling weak, as evidenced by the feeble clunk her boot made against the porch.

"That's enough of that," Veronica said, doing her best to mimic her father's exact tone as she finally looked down at the watch. The pendant's face trembled with the still frantic beating of her heart. Veronica decided to ignore that, too.

"Father's train won't be here for another hour at least," she told herself and the foggy silence. "I shall go up to my room and read while I wait."

Father surely would have scolded her for having voiced her intentions to…empty air, but at the moment Veronica didn't care. Because Father wasn't there to scold.

No one was there.

Except illusions. And flaws in the glass. Things that were to be ignored.

Until they went away.

Giving the window one last quick glance, Veronica pulled the book from the skirt's pocket and clutched it to her blossoming womanhood. Solid. Real. Like a shield.

And it helped. But not a lot.

Especially once she stepped inside the hotel's shadowed foyer.

The ghosts were restless.

It was as though they had been waiting for such an opportunity, when all their living counterparts—save a mere child—were absent. That thought normally would have made Veronica livid, possibly even setting off another foot stamping episode, had she not been concentrating very hard on ignoring the echoing thump of invisible shoes, the clink of tea cups and silverware coming from the empty dining room, the hollow whispers that drifted on the air like dust beaten from a rug…catching only the occasional word or phrase:

"…ewing? Man, now you wanna see nothing but net…"

"…fog…"

"…well, YOU wanted to see sunny california, remember …"

"…eight cents a gallon…shoulda turned that whole friggin' country into nuclear glass when we had the chance …"

"…rush hour…"

"…mutombo…"

"…time share…"

"…hey, anybody want some o.j?…"

It was the howling moan which followed the question that sent Veronica racing up the stairs—

—and straight through the apparition of a woman which suddenly appeared before her.

The ghost, which wore trousers (!) and a baggy shirt advertising the name of the very hotel it was haunting, and like its bearded kinsman from the window, seemed much more surprised than Veronica.

"BE-CAUSE I AM IG-NOR-ING YOU!" she shouted to the rhythm of her unladylike ascent.

It was only when Veronica got to the second story landing, heart pounding against the book, that she finally stopped and turned around. The improperly dressed ghost was gone from the stairs and only silence reigned from below.

Thanks to Father's wise suggestion.

And when Veronica thought she heard the front door open and close twice while she walked down the hallway to her room, she simply ignored it.

As she ignored the tow-headed toddler who appeared without warning and smiled up at her.

As she ignored the lisping "Hi, my name's Bywan. Whad yours?" greeting.

As she tried to ignore the naked bodies entwined upon her bed.

But failed.

Veronica had never seen the human form unclothed

before…even her own, having been told to always keep her eyes averted to Heaven while she bathed…so the sight of the naked ghosts—limbs coiled in such a fashion that she couldn't tell where one body began and the other ended—produced a spontaneous and unexpected reaction.

She laughed. Loudly. The book hitting the floor when the female ghost pushed her spectral lover away and pointed…pointed a trembling finger at Veronica and screamed.

"…oh my god, they were right about this place being haunted…do you see it?…right there…the ghost …"

Veronica turned quickly, her petticoat rustling in spite of their damp overskirt, completely forgetting she was supposed to ignore such things. What ghost? Where? There was nothing behind her, nothing at all save the small writing table and chair beneath the room's solitary window.

A low voice, decidedly male, turned Veronica's attention back to the bed. She could feel another blush rise to her cheeks even though the female ghost was now holding a wrinkled sheet modestly in front of her.

"…hell are you talking about, gail?…"

"…don't tell me you don't see her…"

"…her, who?…"

The female ghost's finger steadied. "…the little girl…she's standing right there…look, she's bending down to pick up something…"

The tip of Veronica's fingers brushed against the book and stopped. When she looked up it was into round green eyes.

"…oh my god, ken…she's looking straight at me…"

"ME?" Veronica gasped, leaving *The Light Princess* to her fate as she stood up. "I'm not a ghost…YOU are!"

"…i think she's trying to communicate, ken…her lips are moving but…i can't hear anything ..."

"This is MY room," Veronica could feel the tendons in her neck quiver as she shouted, trying to pierce the veil between worlds by the force of her exclamation. "And…and I shouldn't even be TALKING to you because…you're not real! You're a flaw, an illusion…a fairy tale and I'm too BIG to believe in—"

"…i wish i could hear her…oh, god, ken…she's crying…"

Veronica raised her hand slowly to her cheek, touched what lay there, then stared at the clear drops left behind on her fingers. Tears?

"…she looks so sad, ken…"

An evil, wicked laugh accompanied the squeak of bedsprings as the male ghost lifted himself to one elbow, leaning forward to pull the sheet away.

"…well, maybe she doesn't know she's dead…" he whispered.

And then they were gone.

Veronica stared at the undisturbed quilt covering her empty bed for a long time before bending down and picking up her book. A pale orange light, the misty harbinger of twilight, began filling the room through the west facing window at her back. Still trembling, Veronica turned to watch the dull vermillion ball that was the setting sun drift slowly down through the thick curtains of fog. Soon, she knew, when the sun's lowest edge touched the sea, the color would change from pale orange to golden pink. Soon…not long now.

Veronica closed her eyes and felt the color shift. There. She'd been at the hotel for so long she almost didn't need a watch to keep track of the passage of time.

How long?

How much time?

…maybe she doesn't know she's dead…

"Content yourself at the hotel, Veronica, and wait for me." Wait for me. Wait.

But for how long?

How long had she been waiting?

When she opened her eyes the room was flooded with muted pink-gold and the bed springs were creaking. She left silently without turning around.

Veronica's steps echoed softly along the empty hall, past the empty rooms, down the empty stairs…drowning out the whispers and thumps and clinks that flitted and circled her head like summer moths.

Like dust.

Like the ticking of the lapel watch.

To be ignored.

Stopping at the bottom of the stairs, tightening her grip on the book, Veronica felt a shiver trace its way down her spine as she looked around. Darkness had crept from its respective daylight abode to lay claim to the foyer and the rooms beyond. Even the tufted velvet settee, her preferred reading place, was crowded with shadows.

When the hotel keeper and his wife returned from town, they would light the lamps and the shadows would depart. And when Father returned she would ...

She would…

Wait for me, Veronica.

I will, Father. Forever.

When something thumped in one of the empty rooms upstairs Veronica looked back over her shoulder and stuck out her tongue.

"I am still ignoring you," she told it, then crossed the foyer on tiptoes, so as to not disturb the shadows, to await her father on the porch.

The call of the gulls was gone, replaced by the dull pounding of wave against rock. Night was coming, already it had painted the edges of fog in shades of lavender and lapis.

It wouldn't be long now, Veronica reminded herself How long?

But just to make sure, she lifted the watch into the fading light and studied the crystal face. Father's train would be arriving in less than a hour and until then she would wait—obedient as the child he thought her still to be.

Shivering as night crowded around her, Veronica sat down on the porch swing and began to read. "Once upon a time…"

GILGAMESH RECIDIVUS

The cold was a living thing, stalking him from the blue shadows, its icy breath encircling his feet as he trudged along the narrow swath of black ice that doubled for a foot-path.

He had never liked the cold—once fearing its final embrace, then seeking it out. For so very long. But now the cold knew him and teased him like a coy lover, allowing him only the slightest touch before scurrying away.

"My, haven't we gotten poetic in our old age," he chided himself, his breath adding another layer of ice to his mahogany-colored beard. "Fool."

Cresting a small rise, he stopped and looked back over his shoulder. The railway village he had left that morning, huge in comparison to most of the Siberian settlements he'd seen dimly through the train's ice-coated windows, had been swallowed by the cold night. If anyone in the village remembered the tall stranger who had stopped only long enough to ask directions of the Station Master, it would be a false memory…one that he had fashioned on the spur of the moment. A new identity. A new name. And a manufactured life to go with it.

He had done it so many times before that it was second nature. So many times before that if he put his mind to it he could almost forget who he really was.

Almost. And never.

Hunching his shoulders beneath the bulky, post-Afghan War parka he had bought from an enterprising black-marketeer, he turned back to the path before him. There was no evidence that another human being had made the same journey since the first snow. The ancient Station Master, once they found a dialect they both could mutilate just enough to understand, had warned him of the outpost's intentional isolation. There would be no one to help him if he became lost. No one to carry him out.

No one to watch him die.

Finally, to die.

He shook his head and laughed, the sound startling the cold away from his face. He had become foolish in his old age. If his journey was successful, he would have more than enough witnesses to his death.

***

While the lieutenant studied the documents that showed a different identity than the one he'd given to the Station Master, he studied the men.

There were three others besides the officer—all identically dressed in the drab brown uniform and woolen great-coat of the Home Guard, each wearing a rabbit fur hat with the ear-flaps down and tied beneath cold-reddened chins. Each with a rifle slung over one shoulder.

A smile tugged at his lips beneath the frost clinging to his beard. He had witnessed this scene so many times before—the self important officer, his soldiers, their weapons—that it gave him a comforting sense of *déjà vu*.

He let the smile fade as the officer looked up. Slumped his shoulders and eased deeper into character. Waited for his cue.

"Bio-genetic engineering," the lieutenant said, nodding as if the term were as familiar to him as the small cast iron stove his men were huddled around.

"Yes," he answered but gave no further explanation. He could have, of course, gone into the most intricate details of gene-splicing—one of the benefits of such a long life was in having the time to learn these things—but, as with his total acquiescence during the soldier's rough handed search, he didn't like to show off.

Unless he had to.

"A very remarkable field. Your papers seem to be in order, however…"

The soldier tapped the forged documents with a gnawed pencil stub and cleared his throat. His accent came from the south; perhaps as far as the Caspian or Black Seas…thousands of kilometers from the Siberian Hell he had been consigned to.

"It must be difficult to be so far from your home, Lieutenant, especially in so inhospitable a place as this."

The soldier looked up through the glare of the kerosene lantern on the desk beside him.

"With such primitive amenities. Don't you miss the sun?"

The narrow face moved away from the light, the almond shaped eyes going from sea-green to azure. The pencil stub pinged when it hit the desk top.

"Why are you here, Doctor…"

"Ambrose," he said, filling in the pause. He'd chosen the name as a final jest…a pun to defy the gods who had abandoned him so long ago.

He didn't realize he'd been smiling until he felt it stop—at the same instant the lieutenant gathered up the documents and placed them in the desk's center drawer. The sound the lock made when it slid home was still echoing in the chilled air when the soldier stood up, his gloved hand going to the thick gunbelt cinched at his waist.

Ambrose took a deep breath and waited. He hadn't planned on killing the men, they were to be his story-tellers. But if their deaths meant that he might finally die ...

He let his hands slowly ball into fists.

"You will be so kind as to tell me how you knew to come to this place, Doctor Ambrose. We are not generally listed in any Intourist publications." The lieutenant's gloved hand moved to the flap on the front of the holster. Ambrose shifted his weight to the balls of his feet. "I suggest you answer now, Doctor. And please…the truth."

You wouldn't accept the truth if I told you, boy.

Sighing, his breath steaming in the frigid air, Ambrose unclenched the fingers of his right hand and reached toward the parka's inside breast pocket. Matching his movements precisely, three SKS-Semi Automatic rifles took aim at his heart.

…if their deaths mean that I can finally die…

No. Not yet.

He lowered the heels of his boots to the wooden floor.

"Peace, friends," he said, more to the lieutenant than to the armed men. "There is an item in my pocket that may explain things to your satisfaction, sir. May I get it?"

A curt nod. "But do so slowly, Doctor Ambrose, the boredom of this place has made my men seek diversion where they can find it."

"Boredom?" He forced his hand to stop at the pocket's lip. "Here? In the presence of the greatest biological discovery of all time? May God forgive your men, lieutenant."

The man's eyes flashed and Ambrose pretended not to notice. The ideological wounds the lieutenant must have suffered when first Communism and then the Marxist Ideal fell were undoubtedly still too fresh for an invocation to God to hold much meaning.

But it will, Ambrose promised silently. By the end of this night it will.

"I must admit that I heard of…this through less than official channels, sir."

Tucking himself deeper into the character of obsessed scientist, Ambrose pulled a five-by-ten centimeter news article and its corresponding photograph from his pocket and laid it on the desk facing the lieutenant. The picture was overexposed and grainy, showing only the vaguest outline of an elongated neck and flowing mane. But the horn was still visible—stark white and pointing straight at heaven like an accusing finger.

"Of course I don't usually buy this sort of journalistic trash," he said, urging his voice into breathless wonder, "but the headline…and picture. My G— Lieutenant, if this story is true then all I need are just a few cells…a simple scraping of the inside of the animal's mouth and…I…I can"

Panting, his breath almost as thick as the frozen mist outside, Ambrose patted his chest and smiled. Weakly. He regretted that with the present government in financial ruin there would be no opportunity to video-tape him. It was the performance of a lifetime. A very long lifetime. And his last performance.

With any luck.

"I apologize, lieutenant," he said sheepishly, still feigning vulnerability, "but I'm sure you can understand my excitement."

The officer grunted as Ambrose leaned forward, compensating for his six-feet, three-inches, and tapped the article with his finger, drawing the man's attention back to it.

The story had appeared in one of the more "reputable" American tabloids, the brazen headline:

RUSSIAN UNICORN DISCOVERED

peaking Ambrose's interest just enough to buy the paper and

suffer the smirks of an overweight supermarket cashier. In lifetimes past, he had discovered that truth, like Edgar Allan Poe's purloined letter, occasionally could only be found where you didn't look for it.

"I know, I know," he went on, "these papers usually tend to vie for the record of Elvis Presley sightings and UFO abduction stories...but you have to understand, lieutenant. If there is any validity to the article—"

His guts twisted over on themselves when the lieutenant looked up.

There was surprise in the man's eyes, yes...naturally, considering the publication...but there was something else as well. Incomprehension. He didn't recognize the animal in the photograph.

Ambrose forced himself to remain calm as the soldier shook his head. Are you gods not done with me yet? It was a lie. Another lie and he should have known better after so many centuries. He almost laughed out loud.

But there was still something about the three other soldiers' nervousness...the way their eyes kept shifting from his face to the small locked door to his left.

The way sweat kept beading upon their brows despite the coldness of the room.

Something.

He sighed, decided to continue the illusion a while longer.

"So." The pain in his voice sounded so real that even he was moved. "I have come all this way in what is usually referred to as a wild goose chase."

"I am familiar with the term, Doctor Ambrose," the lieutenant said, moving his hand from the holster, the chair's frozen springs screaming as he leaned back. "I have not been assigned to Siberia all of my life."

Ah.

Go on, Ambrose. All they can do is shoot at you.

All illusion faded.

"Then why are you here, lieutenant—if the article is false, that is?" He smiled. "I doubt that even a government in transition would assign men to guard an empty Siberian hovel."

His smile was matched.

"I am but a humble officer in the Russian army, Doctor Ambrose," the lieutenant shrugged, "and I do what I am ordered. Without question…even in a transitional government. It is not a lucrative profession, but it keeps food in the bellies of my wife and children."

A man three months in the grave would not have missed the subtle hint. A communist he may have been born and bred, but the lieutenant was willing to make the "sacrifice" to capitalism for the sake of his wife and children.

If he even had a wife and children. Not that Ambrose cared. He had never been a moralist.

Pushing up the left sleeve of his parka, Ambrose quickly removed the gold watch he wore. Time, after so many centuries, meant little to him, and gold was still a highly negotiable commodity.

"Of course, I would not ask for the privilege of seeing what may be behind that locked door without…showing my appreciation."

"Even if there is nothing there, doctor?"

"Even so."

The lieutenant shifted in his chair just enough to hide the transaction from his men and slipped the watch into the front pocket of his great-coat, nodding.

"Then follow me, Doctor Ambrose."

The three soldiers never lowered their rifles as their officer stood up and, taking the kerosene lantern from the desk, led the way across the room. Ambrose imagined the weapons aimed at his back. The sensation reminded him of fleas crawling across his skin; a mild distraction, but of no consequence.

The sound of the hasp opening cracked in the still air…still except for the muffled sound of unshod hooves coming from the darkness beyond the door.

"I cannot give you permission to take anything from the animal, doctor," the lieutenant said, blocking the door with his body, the hand holding the ring of keys again resting upon the holster, "not even a picture, and I apologize for the lack of heat. It—it seems to prefer the cold."

The door opened and Ambrose inhaled the scent of fresh dung and musk and hay. Alive. Whatever was in there was actually alive.

"Stay away from the horn, Doctor," the lieutenant said, standing to one side. "It has already killed one scientist. A biologist, like yourself."

With the light at his back, Ambrose entered the room first.

And froze.

The animal lifted its shaggy head and stared at him through the clouds of steam rising from its nostrils. The light from the lantern turned its dun-colored hide to gold.

The single horn to polished hematite.

It was real.

"I…" For the first time in his life Ambrose did not need to pretend wonder. "I thought from your expression when you saw the photograph that…that it was just another fairy tale."

"It was the picture that confused me, Doctor Ambrose," the lieutenant said, giving the makeshift wooden corral in the center of the room a wide berth as he walked to a work station directly opposite the door. "This animal does not look at all like the one in the photograph."

"No," Ambrose said, "it doesn't."

Tiny and compact, ten hands at the shoulder if that, the Unicorn resembled a stunted Mongolian pony more than the sleek, alabaster creature of myth. Even the horn, pushing its way through the thick forelock, was different. Where the "mythical" alicorn was supposed to be spiraled like that on a narwhal, the "living" horn resembled the protuberance on a rhinoceros. Black as the heart of a Sumerian whore and curved back toward the tufted ears like a scimitar.

Ambrose took a deep breath and let it out as a laugh. It was a hoax. And a pathetic one. Some psychotic veterinarian's idea of a joke. Shifting his eyes, he caught the lieutenant's wide-eyed stare and laughed again.

"My compliments to the designer," he said, tipping his head in a mock bow, "or was this done by committee? That might explain the choice of animal. I'm sure that obtaining an Arab or Lipizzaner, even though it might have looked more like a unicorn, was too much of an expense for the new government to justify. Am I right?"

"You…don't believe what you see?"

Shaking his head, Ambrose walked to the corral and lifted his hand to the animal. Three things happened simultaneously, only two of which he could understand. One was the lieutenant's sudden shout—something about staying away from the corral—the second was the scream coming from the animal itself as it reared up on its hind legs and struck out at the air between them.

The third was the blinding blue light that knocked him to the floor and left behind the smell of ozone and singed horsehide.

—tor Ambrose are you

"— all right?"

Ambrose blinked his eyes and for a moment saw only an afterimage of the animal—its color reversed, finally looking like the fantasy creature it was supposed to be.

"What?"

"We put an electrified grid along the inside of the corral. He, the animal kept...there was no way of holding him without it. The voltage...It isn't capable of hurting him, but he doesn't seem to like it."

I can understand why, Ambrose thought as he allowed the lieutenant to help him to his feet, his own flesh tingling uncomfortably. It was then that he noticed a second gas generator beneath the work station and the thick cable that ran from it to the corral. A bright red alligator clamp attached the cable to the chicken wire mesh that had been nailed to the inside of the wooden railing. It seemed a makeshift design, but very effective.

Ambrose felt a drop of moisture touch his chin an instant before it refroze and wondered exactly how high the voltage was, even though the lieutenant was right about it not seeming to affect the animal.

The Unicorn had settled down, shaking its brush-like mane and pawing at the trampled straw. That, at least, Ambrose noticed, concurred with the legend. The hoof, although almost completely covered with thick, black "feathers", was cloven like a goat's.

Like those he had once seen being woven into a tapestry.

So long ago.

"I can understand the need for such security measures, Lieutenant," he said. "You certainly don't want anyone to get near enough to see the suture marks around the horn or study the surgically altered hooves."

Brushing off his sleeve where the man's hand had been, Ambrose turned and began walking to the door. "Thank you for your time. And the side-show."

"This is no side-show, Doctor Ambrose."

It was the way the lieutenant said those words that made Ambrose stop and walk back to within an inch of the corral. At that distance, he could hear the electricity humming through the wire mesh—could feel it prickle the hair on his arms and legs even through his clothing. His beard and eyebrows felt like they were standing at attention.

"Watch," the lieutenant said.

And Ambrose watched.

Watched the lieutenant remove the sidearm from its holster and take aim at the animal. Watched, with a sensation of compressed time, the bullet leave the muzzle and tear a hole in the quivering chest.

Watched, too, as the shredded flesh curled back in around the wound and closed.

The Unicorn snorted and pawed the ground, undisturbed by either the shot or the armed soldiers running into the room.

"It is all right," the lieutenant told his men, "I was just giving the doctor a demonstration. Dismissed."

Ambrose only heard the sounds of their boots striking the wooden flooring as they left. He couldn't take his eyes off the animal. Didn't dare.

"By the gods. How...old is it?"

He could hear the lieutenant replace the handgun and snap the holster flap back in place.

"The Biologist...the one who was killed...wasn't sure, he never got a chance to collect much data. But he thought it was old. Very old."

"Is it immortal?" Ambrose whispered.

This time it was the lieutenant who laughed.

"Of course not, doctor. No. Nothing is immortal."

"Are you so sure?"

The smile faltered slightly around the edges. "Yes, Doctor, I am. This animal was found in one of the most hostile environments known to man. It's only natural that it would…develop certain natural survival skills that our scientists haven't encountered before."

"Yes," Ambrose said, looking again at the animal's barrel chest. Where the bullet had impacted the hair had reformed in the shape of a star. "I would think that spontaneous tissue repair is not something most scientists deal with on a regular basis. How then do they explain it? Or the animal?"

The lieutenant's grin acquired some of its former glory.

"I'm sorry, Doctor, but the tour is over." Nodding once, he spun on his heels and walked to the work table. His gloved fingers were closing around the lantern's wire handle when the unicorn suddenly nickered.

Ambrose backed away from the corral and into the lengthening shadows as the lieutenant crossed the room. The cold fingered his throat as he unzipped the parka.

"Ah, do you hear that, Doctor Ambrose?" The lieutenant asked, increasing the lamp's brightness. The shadows slunk back and Ambrose joined them. "That moaning sound? It's only the wind, but sometimes out here a man can imagine…many things. A storm is coming and our friend here wants to be out in it. We found him in a storm, did the newspaper mention that? No? Oh, well. It's that sound, I think…it's like it calls to him." A shudder passed over the lieutenant's bowed shoulders. "Foolishness. Now, doctor, if you would be so kind to accompany me back to my desk I can—"

The shock in the lieutenant's eyes bordered on fear when he turned and found himself staring at Ambrose's naked form. Darkness crept closer as the lantern made a shaky decent to the floor. Ambrose followed the dark, closing the gap between them.

Underlit, the lieutenant's face took on the visage of a death mask.

Ambrose nodded his head. It was a good omen.

"It is not so foolish to hear voices in the wind, Lieutenant," he said, feeling the cold wrap itself around him like a lover. "That is how the gods speak to men. And drive them mad."

"HERE!" The lieutenant shouted and, like the well trained dogs they were, the soldiers came running.

Ambrose felt the sensation of fleas tickling his spine once more. And smiled.

Lifting his hands away from his sides, he glanced back over his shoulders, just to make sure his instincts hadn't failed him after so many centuries. They hadn't. The rifles were level and not even a blind man could miss at that distance. The smile grew.

"Get his clothes and handcuff him to one of the chairs out there!" The lieutenant seemed less afraid now, with the men in the room. Or maybe it was the rifles that made him brave. "Then call down to the village and have them send someone to take him off our hands. I don't want this pervert here any longer than he needs to be."

Ambrose lifted his chin, the smile fading as he closed his eyes as one set of boots began moving toward him.

"No," he commanded.

The boots stopped.

He opened his eyes and saw beads of sweat on the lieutenant's face.

The unicorn was prancing nervously within its electrified enclosure—tossing its head, the lantern light flashing across the midnight horn.

It knows.

"Wh-what do you want?" the lieutenant asked, his voice almost lost to the howl of the wind.

Ambrose nodded. "You're direct. I've always

appreciated that and will answer in kind. I've come to kill the unicorn."

"NO!" Despite his obvious fear, the officer placed himself between Ambrose and the corral. Gun coming clumsily to his hand. Shaking. One more inch and the back of his great-coat would brush against the electric mesh. "Are you mad? You saw for yourself that it can't be killed. This is the last of its kind...you can't kill it. Besides, I'm not afraid of a crazy man. I warn you, Doctor, that if you take one more step toward this creature I will kill you."

Smiling, Ambrose took that step.

And the room exploded with sound.

He heard and memorized each one: The trumpeting scream of the unicorn, the paper-tearing riiippp of the assault rifles, the hollow thump as bullets punched holes through his body.

The wet sound of retching as the bloodless wounds repaired themselves as fast as the unicorn's had.

Finally, a whisper.

"Who are you?"

Looking down, he ran a hand over his unmarked flesh; brushing away the last remnants of the Ambrose impersonation.

When he looked back up, Gilgamesh smiled at the lieutenant.

"Just an old man who has grown tired of living," he said gently, using the tone he remembered from countless story telling and lullabies. "If I am successful in killing the unicorn then I may find the secret of killing myself. Or, perhaps the unicorn will kill me..." He took a deep breath and listened to the storm's growing rage. "Either way I shall be dead."

The lieutenant took another step toward the corral, sobbing now, shaking his head.

"No. Y-you can't."

"What do you mean? Kill or be killed? I have done so much of the former that it means nothing. And as for the latter…"

Gilgamesh closed his eyes, trying to blot out the memories, but they were still there—as fresh and solid as if he were living through them at that very moment. Again.

"Read the legends if you want about a man not much older than yourself who so feared death that he usurped the powers of the gods.

"See a plant that gave eternal life. You would look for such a thing, wouldn't you?" he asked through the darkness of his closed eyes, not expecting an answer. Getting none. "Of course you would. Any man terrified of death would."

When Gilgamesh finally opened his eyes, he didn't look at the man, only watched the animal. The unicorn was calm—neck arched, heavy tail swatting lazily at its golden sides, ears pitched forward as if it too were listening.

"Imagine then finding out how much you have given up to become immortal…the last of your kind…to see all that you ever loved wither and fade to dust while you stand forever unchanged."

Smiling as he once had smiled at a precocious carpenter's son in Jerusalem, Gilgamesh reached over and removed the empty gun from the limp hand.

"I will tell you another secret, Lieutenant," he whispered. "That part of the legend where the serpent is supposed to carry off the plant of eternal life is wrong. It never did.

The look on the man's face had shifted from fear to confusion. Gilgamesh chuckled softly.

"Forgive an old man his digressions, lieutenant," he said and tossed the gun into the shadows at the far end of the room. When it struck the floor, the unicorn shied and the ends of its tail bushed against the wire. Blue sparks danced across the mesh.

"I'm sorry," Gilgamesh said, not sure whether he meant to address man or unicorn. "Please, stand aside, Lieutenant, and let me give the story the ending it deserves."

Round eyes the color of broken ice met his.

"You're out of your mind," the Lieutenant screamed over the building storm. "Legends can't die."

"Why not?" Gilgamesh asked as the man swung at him.

He hadn't meant to protect himself, there was no need—blows were as meaningless as bullets—but he did. Gilgamesh caught the man's closed fist and pushed. He reacted, and heard the gods laugh.

"NO!"

But it was already too late.

A halo of blue-white flame blossomed around the lieutenant's body as he fell backwards into the wire. Steam and sparks, the color of urine in the lantern light, erupted from the generator beneath the work table as the overloaded circuits shut down.

Silence. For a moment. And then the muffled sound of cloven hooves on straw. Building up speed.

The unicorn's back hoof shattered the lantern as it leapt over its smoldering protector and charged.

Gilgamesh felt the same jolt of energy he had experienced when he had accidentally brushed against the electric barrier, but this was a hundred times worse. It drained him instantly.

Collapsing, Gilgamesh rolled into a ball and groaned. It felt as if all the centuries he'd lived through had finally caught up with him.

He was panting, barely able to hear the hysterical shouting of the soldiers above the pounding of his own heart.

No...it wasn't his heart...his heart hadn't beat in two millennium. Lifting himself to one elbow, Gilgamesh watched through growing flames as the tiny, dun-colored unicorn cocked its hind legs and kicked out another wall plank.

The building was old, probably constructed in haste against the coming of a long past winter, its timbers rotted. In less time than it took Gilgamesh to push away from the hungry fire, the unicorn was free.

He thought he heard it once...whinnying its triumph to an uncaring sky...but it might have been only the storm. The gods laughing at his defeat.

Again.

The flames were already feeding on the dead lieutenant when Gilgamesh was finally able to stand. The clothes he had worn to the outpost had been the fire's first course, but that didn't matter; if there were no extra uniforms in the building he would simply "appropriate" one from its current owner. Being just another faceless soldier in a country still tottering from years of suppression would make it easier to track the unicorn.

To find it and—

He stumbled over a crack in the floor and pitched forward, grabbing the door frame to keep from falling. Oh yes, tracking down the unicorn would be child's play compared to simply walking out of the building.

Then he noticed his hand in the wash of firelight.

It looked different.

He raised the second and turned them slowly from back to front. They were different.

His hands had always been a source of pride to him—smooth and strong enough to crack two hard-shelled nuts or a man's skull; but the hands before him now were wrinkled flesh, the fingers knobbed and curled in toward the palm.

Gilgamesh stretched out his fingers as far as they would go and watched them tremble.

They were the hands of an old man.

Old.

He didn't have to feel his face or look down at the sagging flesh that hung from his limbs. He knew. He had aged.

From one brief touch, the unicorn had leeched away centuries.

Throwing back his head, suddenly lighter from its lack of hair, Gilgamesh laughed until the sound caught in his throat and tried to strangle him. So this was what it felt like to be old. He didn't care much for it, but it was a start.

Pushing away from the heat-blistered door frame, Gilgamesh shuffled through the empty outer office and into the howling night. A naked old man wandering through a storm would be a pitiable sight to anyone who saw it, but he knew there would be no one foolish enough to venture out on a night like this. And if one did, he would have clothing and a new identity—either by guile or the knife, which ever was easiest.

He was even less worried about the dead lieutenant's men. They were probably already half way back to town.

With stories to tell about the unicorn and the stranger who appeared as if by magic and could not be killed.

The stuff of which legends were made.

Bracing himself against the howling cold, Gilgamesh faced into the worst of the storm. It would be hours…days more than likely…before any of the town's people braved the elements…and story…to come up this far. By then the building would be nothing more than snow covered ash—whatever truth it held burned away. The tracks left by his bare feet and the unicorn's hooves long since buried beneath the drifts.

Just another story to keep the children from wandering too far into the woods.

Just another joke played on a tired, old man.

Gilgamesh raised his fists to the storm just as something moved through the wind-driven snow directly ahead of him, a living shadow—its body the color of old cream, its ebony mane and tail whipping shadows out of the lighter colored storm…the scimitar horn rising into the night as the shadow creature reared.

"WAIT!" he shouted, pleading with it as he opened his arms. "COME BACK!"

The shadow dissolved.

"You aren't finished with me yet," he yelled, looking past the skuttering clouds to the blackness beyond. "Are you?"

Only the wind moaned an answer.

Ignoring the cold, Gilgamesh hunched his bony shoulders and headed north, away from the tiny knot of civilization and into the empty Siberian wastelands.

Following…the…unicorn.

Back into legend.

ANCIENT ONE

Only an hour from the birthing bed, the young woman pushed back a curling lock of sweat matted hair and walked—slowly…painfully—to the tiny wooden cradle in front of the banked fire.

Winter seemed to take pity on her that night, calming the northern wind even as her child's mewling howl filled the hut. It was a blessing, the woman thought again as she looked down at the now sleeping babe. So many things could have gone wrong…so many things had gone wrong. Before.

The woman took a deep breath and carefully lowered herself to the thick ram's fleece on which the cradle sat, pushing away the memories of babes born the color of Robin eggs the way she pushed another lock of hair from her face.

He was perfect. Strong and healthy and with a cry that even startled the mid-wife, so lusty it had been.

He would live.

"Please," the woman whispered and grasped the heavy cross laying at her breasts, hoping the silent god of the black hooded monks was close enough to hear. "If yer real'y there, m'lord…'ave pity on m'poor babe."

The wind whispered around the hide-and-bone door covering, but the new god remained silent.

The woman dropped her hand from the cross as the mid-wife returned from burying the birthing sheets.

"Ye'd do bett'r t'speak t'th' auld uns," the mid-wife hissed, eyes narrowing in the firelight's glow, "an' burn a sprig'a mistletoe so they'll not take this un like they took t'others."

The new mother's hands fluttered to her lips as the mid-wife's words…and their meaning…lowered themselves over her shoulders like a clinging mist. Despite her precautions and sacrifices, the Auld Ones had taken her babes before they'd so much as drew breath; what would they think now that she wore a newcomer's charm around her throat?

Her frightened whimper became a thin scream as a hunched, cloaked figure pushed the door covering to one side and stamped into the hut.

"What pratt'l ye be spoutin' now, w'man?" the figure growled as it slowly began peeling the layers of sodden wool from around its broad shoulders. "Nay more sense then sheep bleetin'."

The new mother felt the wild beating of her heart slow as the dim firelight showed the unexpected visitor to be her man's father. It was only when the heavy woolen cloak lay against the hearth stones that the old man finally looked down at his son's son.

"Does he bide well?"

Smiling, the new mother placed her hand to cradle and smiled.

"He does," she said, wanting to add he lives but was afraid to in case the silent new god wasn't as powerful as the Auld Ones. "He does well."

The old man grunted and turned back to the fire to warm his hands.

"Ah tol' her t'burn a sprig'a mistletoe," the mid-wife huffed as she wound her own cloak around her shoulders. "Be worth more'n that thing hangin' round her neck."

"An' what would a sheep know o'worth," the old man said without turning. "Run 'long home now, ya ol'ewe, ah'll mind th' watch."

The mid-wife left without another word, except to hiss something into the wind that might have been a blessing or a curse as she entered the night. Almost at the same instant the wind began to scream across the fens like a hundred damned souls and winter returned.

"Just th' wind," the old man told his son's wife as if he knew the fear coating her heart with ice. "An' wind ne'r hurt th' livin'."

The new mother looked down at her sleeping babe and quickly covered her face with both hands.

"If he lives," she whispered, the words tearing at her throat like the teeth of carding combs. "Ah prayed t' th' new god...if the Auld Ones were listenin' ..."

Her man's father threw back his head and laughed loud enough to wake the babe. Both were bald and both seemed surprised at the sound the other was making.

"Eh? Nay, this'un'll live t'see his own babes havin' babes." The woman heard the old man's knees pop as he kneeled next to the cradle. "Jus' listen t'him."

"But th' Auld Ones might take offense at m'prayin' t'th' new god ..."

This time the old man's laughter was soft. "Gods got bett'r things t'do then listen t'th' likes o'us. Ah...but will ye listen t'him now. Nay, if he makes it through this night he'll make it through many a'more."

The woman inched closer to the cradle and wrapped her arms around its rough hewed sides.

"Whatta mean?" she gasped. "Ye just said—"

The old man's face stopped the words in her throat like a cork in a bottle.

"Listen, girl," he said as he drew something small

and brown from the loose folds of his tunic, "it weren't no god that took yer babes, 'twas a curse set down on m'father's father fer a wrong he did a wise'n holy woman.

"He kilt her babe an' the'curse was set…for his line t'die out." When he saw the terror growing in her tired eyes, he smiled and cupped the thing he held in his hand gently. "If it weren't fer this, nary would ah be sittin' here talkin' t'ye…an' nary would ye be sittin' here listen'n."

He handed her the thing and watched her take it with trembling fingers, turning it first one way and then the other. In the fire's glow, the brown sheep's wool looked like polished amber.

"What it be?" the woman asked, one finger tracing the rawhide stitched mouth and black stone eyes. "A man?"

"Nay," the old man said, taking it back and laying it next to his sleeping grandchild, "'tis a protector. It'll protect th' babe from what may come in th' night.

"'Twasn't able t'help yer other babes," he said, setting the cradle to rocking, "bein' born dead as they were, bu' this un…this bonny un'll live t'see th' morn.

"Th' ancient one'll see t'it. Now," the old man said, taking the woman's hands and pulling her to her feet, "ye need yer rest if ye plan t'nurse my grandchild come th'-morn."

She seemed to have barely enough strength to walk to the pile of sleeping skins let alone argue, and for that the old man was grateful. If she were to see the things that would come for her babe …

He felt himself tremble and covered it quickly with a forced chuckle.

"Have ye no fear, li'l mamma," he said as he lowered her into the skins, "ah'll fetch ye if he starts caterwaulin' fer his supper."

She fell into an exhausted sleep almost immediately.

The old man stood watching her for a moment, his hand straying to the polished stone around his neck, before turning back to the fire.

And the sleeping babe.

And to what might come in the night.

The ancient protector seemed to wink at him from the growing darkness.

***

Edwina Farris nee-Terbow folded the alabaster tissue back over her father-in-law's gift and shook her head.

"Oh, Bertram, no." Setting the cerulean colored box aside, she straightened the lace collar of her bed jacket and touched the flat of her hand to her hair. "I'm afraid it simply won't do. I don't see how your father would think it an appropriate gift for…our son."

It was impossible for Bertram not to have noticed his wife's reluctance to use their child's chosen name—undoubtedly because she had not been given a choice in the choosing. Anymore then he had.

A note had come back from his father in response to his own "Edwina has taken to her bed. Birth appears imminent" missive; the familiar flowing script as direct (and cold) as the old man himself.

"Duncan Trahern if it is a son. Lavinia Brenna for a girl."

The choices had made Bertram glad his first child had had the good sense to be born male.

Taking the gift that had followed the note by an hour after, Bertram carried it to the brass bassinet and brushed back the tulle drape. Smiled down at the wrinkled little face and imagined he could see a little of himself in the sleep puffed eyes and downy red fluff peeking out from under the satin bonnet.

Duncan Trahern Farris.

Their son.

His son.

Bertram felt his chest swell against the silk evening vest he wore.

"You really will have to speak to your father, Bertie," his wife said as he dropped the drape and turned. "That…thing is absolutely not acceptable."

Having only gotten the merest of glances before his wife folded the tissue back over it, Bertram lifted the box into the soft yellow glow of the gas-light and fingered the paper apart.

And gasped.

In delight.

"Good God," he almost shouted, then, remembering his son (his son) instantly dropped his voice to a whisper as he stared at the thing in his hands, "I can't believe it."

"I know," his wife sniffed, readjusting the eyelet spread over her legs, "it is just too…provincial to consider keeping. We'd be the laughing stock of all our friends. No, it really is too much. First he decides on a name for our child and then…this monstrosity. No. I'll not have it in the same room as my child. And with all his money, too. It's inexcusable. You'll have to speak with him, Bertie."

Bertram mumbled a "Yes, dear. Of course, dear" as he lifted the threadbare toy from its box. A length of satin ribbon, crimson and gaudy, had been tied into a jaunty bow around the nipped in neck.

Dropping the box to the carpet, Bertram lifted the gift to his face and buried his nose into its soft belly. The musky, all but forgotten scent filled his head.

"Bertram!" His wife shouted from across the room. "How can you? That…thing doesn't look…wholesome."

Lowering it from his face, Bertram pressed a thumb against first one, then the other black stone eye before running it across the stitched-in smile; before bending back one of the nubby "ears" and finding the white thread stitches his mother had used to sew up the evidence of his often heavy-handed childish devotion.

He felt his own smile match the stitched one as he looked up. With the exception of the bright new ribbon, the toy was exactly as he remembered it.

"Do you know what this is," he asked softly.

His wife folded her hands primly over the slight bulge still evident at her waist and lifted her chin.

"I have already told you what I think it is, Bertram," she said stiffly. "It is a monstrosity and your father should be made to feel ashamed for having sent it to his first grandchild. I expect you to see to that."

For the first time during their five year marriage, Bertram ignored his wife's cold expectations of him and carried the gift back to his son.

"BERTRAM! Don't you dare put that…thing in with our son! It may be…diseased."

"Edwina, it is not diseased and it is not a thing. And our son shall have it." Pushing back the drape a second time, Bertram placed the toy next to his sleeping son. "It's my old teddy."

An icy "humph" drifted across the room to him. He ignored that as well.

"It doesn't look much like a teddy," his wife said. "Your family apparently was less well off than it is today."

Bertram snuggled the toy in closer to his son before letting the drape close and turning around..

"On the contrary," he said, "my family has always

been well off...unlike other families I may mention."

The narrowing of her eyes told him that his remark had indeed hit its mark. "All the more reason to refuse it, don't you think? A hand-me-down for our first child..."

"More than a hand-me-down," Bertram said. "More like an antique. Been in the family for generations, I was told...from father to son to each of that generation's progeny." He chuckled as he walked toward his wife's bed, stopping—prudently—at one of the chairs that had been set up for visitors. "I remember how I cried the night my little brother was born and Father took Oldie from me...that was my name for him because he was so old, you see.

"I didn't sleep very well that night—I believe I missed the comfortable warmth of him—and was quite resentful, I was afraid of Clayborne's growing attachment to my teddy." His smile grew as his wife's mouth tightened into a thin frown. "After that I believed the teddy went on to Jocelyn then to Taybor ..."

He shrugged. "This is the first time I've even thought of my old friend in almost thirty years."

His wife appeared not the least bit interested.

"It is still a miserly gift to give our son, Bertram."

Knowing his wife as well as he did, Bertram Rowan Farris folded his hands over one raised knee and nodded.

"Perhaps," he said, "but it will make a good impression on his grandfather who, I dare say, will then shower our son with gifts that might even put the Magi's offerings to shame."

Status, if not reason, had its desired effect upon his wife's heart.

"As you think best, Bertie," she said.

***

"For the new baby?" Little Fiona asked as she watched her mother stitch a pink satin heart to the front of her old teddy. She hadn't played with it since getting the china head Baby Doll for Christmas the year before, but seeing it—laying across her mother's aproned knees, a bright new heart covering the bald patch she herself had rubbed in its belly—made her own tummy feel funny.

Made her want it back.

"But it's mine," she said, reaching out to touch the nubby feeling fur. "Mine."

Her mother pulled the teddy out of reach as she snapped the pale pink thread between her fingers.

"But you have so many prettier things, Fee. Can't your new little brother have just this one old thing?"

Fiona looked at her China Baby Dolly, sitting straight legged and proper in front of the miniature tea cup and tiny plate filled with cracker crumbs and felt her bottom lip tremble.

"No," she whined, "Old Bear's mine! Don't want Brion to have him!"

But before Fiona could take him back, her mother stood up—slowly—taking Old Bear along with her. Fiona suddenly felt very, very small.

"I already explained to you, Fee," her mother said from her great height above Fiona's upturned face. "It's a family tradition…the newest baby in the family always gets Old Bear. Remember, I told you that before the baby came. Remember?"

Fiona remembered something about being told she wasn't going to be the baby of the family anymore but couldn't remember anything about having to give Old Bear away.

Didn't WANT to remember.

"Don't want …" she started as her mother walked away; walked toward the long, dark staircase that led upstairs.

To her new baby brother.

"…Old Bear to go. He's mine!"

Her mother stopped when she got to the bottom step and took a deep breath, looked back at Fiona and shook her head.

"You're being a very selfish little girl, Fiona Margaret," her mother said, pressing Old Bear to her chest as she lifted herself up the carpeted steps. "You have a perfectly beautiful baby doll that cost your father dearly…especially in these hard times…with the talk of war with Germany while children are going hungry in the streets …"

Fiona watched Old Bear bounce against her mother's chest as she moved higher into the darkness that lay above.

"I'm going to tell your father about your selfishness, Fiona," her mother said, little more than a piece of the darkness herself, "you just wait and see if I don't, missy. Whining like a baby…well, you'd best understand that you're not a baby anymore and start acting accordingly. So many children going hungry. It's family tradition that the baby gets Old Bear and that's the end of it. I don't want to hear another word. Old Bear is Brion's now and that's the way it will be…until another one comes along…Go…play …with…your…baby…while ...

"you…still…

"can."

Her mother's voice got softer and softer until Fiona couldn't make out the words. Just the sounds. Coming from her parent's room.

Where the new baby was.

Where Old Bear was.

Pouting, Fiona turned and walked back to where her baby doll sat, stiff legged and perfect, waiting for the Tea Party to begin. The China Doll was beautiful, with blue eyes and golden hair painted in spit-curls around the cherub like face.

She was much better than Old Bear.

Prettier.

Smarter.

Colder.

She wouldn't know what to do when the monsters came back in the night.

The pout trembled along Fiona's lips as she kicked the baby doll over and crushed its perfectly beautiful face beneath the sole of her shoe.

***

"Ack-ack-ack-ack! Lookie me, Grandpa Duncan, lookie me…I'm a fighter plane…ack-ack-ack-ack. Gonna get them dirty Japs…Lookie, Grandpa Duncan!"

Jamie held his arms straight above his head and "flew" Cedric into the side of his Grandfather's leg. Cedric, used to such abuse since the telegram had come explaining how Daddy's ship had gone down fighting the Japs, continued to smile—his bright black eyes gleaming red, blue, green, yellow as Jamie changed directions and sent him on a bombing mission toward the Christmas tree.

"Gonna get them Japs that got Daddy, Grandpa Duncan…lookie!"

Grandpa Duncan's big hand closed over Jamie's shoulder, cutting short Cedric's mission to get all the dirty Japs.

"Come here, Jamie," the old man said and before Jamie could protest that, at seven, he was too old to be cuddled (even though it felt good) he found himself engulfed. "You're the man of the house now. You know that, don't you?"

Despite the fact that he was "too old" and now "the man of the house," Jamie settled against his grandfather's tobacco-scented warmth and nodded. And then (without knowing why he was doing it) tucked his thumb into his mouth as he pulled Cedric into the hollow beneath his chin.

"Ah, so hard to lose a father," the old man sighed, his great chest shivering as it deflated, "harder even than losing a son. But you're the man now, Jamie…Do you think you're ready for that responsibility?"

Jamie popped the thumb out of his mouth and nodded, Cedric's thin, wooly fur tickling the crook of his neck. He'd heard a lot about "responsibility" since his Mama had gotten the pale yellow telegram—heard it from the neighbors and Father Dunnigan and his aunts and uncles and especially from Grandpa Duncan.

"Good. Very good," the old man said.

Then he did a very strange thing. He lifted Cedric from Jamie's hand and held him up to the light. Surrounded by the glow of Christmas lights, Jamie thought his old teddy bear looked like one of the Saints in the church's stained glass windows. This time it was Jamie who sighed. Contentedly.

"This is…Cedric?" Grandpa Duncan asked, then chuckled so softly that if it wasn't for his chest jiggling up and down Jamie wouldn't have known. "I called him Arthur…after King Arthur of the Round Table. Silly, I suppose, but I used to pretend he really was a knight in shining armor that would protect me from any dragon that happened along.

"Do you pretend that sort of thing with old Cedric here?"

Jamie nodded even though it wasn't dragons that

Cedric protected him from, it was the creeping shadows that came out from under his bed. Sometimes. At night.

But when Jamie reached out to reclaim the raggedy teddy, Grandpa Duncan lowered it quickly below the arm of the chair.

"I was a little younger than you are now," Grandpa Duncan said, tightening his grip around Jamie's shoulders to keep him from squirming after the toy, "when my brother Everett, that's your Great Uncle Everett, was born. I remember that night even after all these years, Jamie…my father, your Great-Grandpa Bertram, coming into my room and whispering that I had a new baby brother. I wasn't much impressed by the news, I remember…probably the same way you feel about your new baby sister…

"Isn't that right, Jamie?"

Jamie squirmed out of his grandfather's grip just far enough to look back over his shoulder to the closed door of his Mother's room. She was in there with the NEW BABY. Resting, Grandpa Duncan had told him, because having a baby is very hard on a woman and that's why she couldn't get up to fix Jamie's supper or play with him or read to him or count the first stars that came out or listen to *Little Orphan Annie* and *Terry and the Pirates* or any of the other things they did every night.

Jamie would have kept watching the door if Grandpa Duncan hadn't hooked one finger under his chin and turned him around.

"So many new responsibilities…no father and now a new little sister to take care of. Do you think you can handle all that, Jamie?"

He nodded and looked for Cedric. He wasn't in his grandfather's hand anymore.

"Where's Cedric? We gotta count the stars."

Grandpa Duncan sighed and patted Jamie's knee.

"Arthur and I used to count raindrops," he chuckled, "but all that stopped when I gave him to Everett. Just like your counting stars will stop when you give Cedric to your new little sister."

"Uh uh," Jamie said, wiggling off the old man's lap. Darting around to the side of the chair, he snatched Cedric up from the floor and tucked him carefully beneath his arm. "Cedric's gotta go fight dirty Japs."

Jamie wasn't sure which surprised him the most—the tiny airplane that Grandpa Duncan suddenly pulled out of his coat pocket or the way his grandfather snatched Cedric out of his hand.

Still wasn't sure even when Grandpa Duncan pressed the plane into Jamie's empty hand and stood up.

"It's for the best," the old man said as he walked to the closed door of his mother's room. "You'll see that in a few years…we all do. Your own father cried for a week when he had to give…Ah, never mind. You're a big boy now, Jamie, too big to be sleeping with a teddy. Too big…and your sister is so tiny and helpless."

Grandpa Duncan turned when he got to the door and winked. "A plane's much better for fighting dirty Japs, anyway. You're a good boy, Jamie. A very good boy."

Then the old man opened the door and carried Cedric in to the NEW BABY.

Jamie stood there for a long time, holding the tiny plane and watching the closed door and trying not to cry because he was "the man of the family" now.

And, as he stood there, he decided he hated the NEW BABY.

It was so cold!

Jamie couldn't remember it ever being that cold in the apartment before. Or that dark. But he'd never been up that late before. Never.

And it'd been hard. Especially without Cedric to protect him from the creeping shadows. Even though he hadn't seen any as he slipped from his bed and tip-toed down the hall to his mother's room, Jamie knew they were there…just waiting for him…because he didn't have Cedric to protect him.

He needed Cedric. The NEW BABY didn't. SHE had mother to watch over her. HE had no one.

Now.

But he would.

Soon.

Jamie held his breath as he opened the door to his mother's room, pausing for a moment to listen to Grandpa Duncan's loud snoring from the couch before creeping into the cold, softly-lit room.

His mother had taken out his old night-light and set it up on the high dresser. For the NEW BABY, she'd told Jamie when they got it out of the cardboard box in the closet…long before the NEW BABY had even shown up. Even before the pale yellow telegram had come telling them about Daddy and the dirty Japs.

Jamie chewed on his lower lip as he tip-tip-toed over to the little bed (that had been HIS, too) next to the radiator.

Cedric was there, snuggled in beside the NEW BABY, the heart shaped bald spot on his tummy glowing white in the almost dark.

It made Jamie MAD.

Moving slowly, prepared to pull back if his mother suddenly sat up and asked him what he was doing, Jamie reached in between the wooden slats of HIS old bed and grabbed one of Cedric's stubby arms. And since he was "the man of the house", he left behind the shiny new airplane Grandpa Duncan had given him…just to show the NEW BABY he wasn't too mad.

With Cedric safely pressed to his chin, Jamie tip-tip-toed back to his own room and, shivering because he thought he'd seen the creeping shadows in his mother's room, crawled back under the covers.

He was almost asleep when the screaming started.

At first Jamie thought it was an Air-raid Siren…like the ones that went off every Friday morning…then he heard the words.

And felt the cold night settle down over him.

"CORLISS! OH-MY-GOD NO! NO! CORLISS PLEASE GOD NOT HER TOO…NOT HER…NO NO…NO…NO…NO…NO…NO!"

Then there was a thumping sound—feet pounding across the floor and the slam of a door being thrown open. A deeper voice, rumbling like distant thunder, was trying to stop the screams. But it wasn't working.

Jamie could still hear the siren like screams.

Could feel the cold wrap itself tighter around him as he slid from his bed and crept down the hall.

To his mother's room.

His mother was sitting on the edge of the bed—hair tangled through her fingers as she rocked back and forth, back and forth, the screams coming each time she rocked. Back and forth. Grandpa Duncan stood next to her, patting her shoulders, talking softly, trying to get her to stop.

Back and forth. Back and forth.

Something small and still and wrapped in a pale blanket lay on his mother's bed. It rolled boneless from side to side as his mother rocked.

Back and forth. Back and forth. The NEW BABY rolled back and forth.

"Mama?" Jamie said softly and waited for them to notice him standing there.

The howling screams were almost as bad as the look on Grandpa Duncan's face when he saw Cedric in Jamie's arms.

…almost…

***

James watched as his daughter-in-law swept through the living room, the flowing skirt and sleeves of her Anti-Apartheid caftan moving in time with the "Songs of the Wolf" CD playing softly in the background and marveled again at the strength of modern women.

Only six hours after the birth of his granddaughter and she was moving as if she'd just gotten back from jogging. Amazing. His own mother had been confined to her bed for nearly a week after the birth of his little ...

James lifted the highball glass to his lips and tried to drown the memory under waves of Scotch.

"Fix you another, Dad?" his son, Kevin, asked. "After all, we've got a lot of celebrating to do. Isn't every day your first granddaughter is born."

"Thank God," M'Lyssa, Kevin's wife, said as she wandered back into the room. It'd been her third trip to the nursery—this time to make sure the Baby Monitor was working—since coming home from the hospital.

An hour earlier.

James shook his head at the wonder of modern post-natal care (or lack of it) and handed his empty glass to his son.

"A little more soda this time, please, Kev…Another as strong as the last and you'll be having a house guest for the night."

James pretended he hadn't seen the "look" that passed between his son and daughter-in-law. No one wanted a doddering old man around…especially not with a brand new baby in the house.

Especially not the first night home.

As he'd ignored the "look", James ignored the sudden chill that pricked the hair at the back of his neck.

"Ah," he said instead, "aren't planning on having another one for a while?"

"Never," M'Lyssa said, coming to rest momentarily on the non-rain forest frame of their Futon couch. "Kevin and I gave the current world situation serious thought before we conceived Tiffany and decided, as responsible adults in an already overpopulated world, that one child per couple was only reasonable."

"Uh huh. And what do you think about all that, Kev?"

His son shrugged. James hadn't expected anything else.

Ever since the raven haired woman-child had dug her claws into his son their last year of college, she—of the hyphenated name—had either countermanded or completely disregarded any idea that hadn't first been cleared by the Mother Earth Society.

Much like she had disregarded James suggestion of a name. Tara for a girl or Tyler for a boy. Good, strong, family names that wouldn't suffer that much from being "modernized."

Tara or Tyler. And he got a Tiffany.

Well, at least they kept it in the same alphabetical drawer.

It was that (and the two scotches he'd already had) that made James accept the third drink with a frown.

"You're seriously considering not having more children, Kev? Seriously?"

Another shrug; James watched his only son—after four daughters—scoot into the vacant spot next to his wife.

"Don't have much choice, Dad," he said. "I had a vasectomy when M'Lyss began her second tri-mester."

James downed the drink without feeling it, wishing he hadn't asked for so much water.

"And what would have happened," he asked when the fluid finally cleared his throat, "if M'Lyssa had lost the baby?"

This time two pair of shoulders shrugged.

"Then it would have meant the baby wasn't supposed to be born…" M'Lyssa said, with the solid conviction of a woman who'd just given birth to a healthy child. "Did you hear that? Excuse me a minute—"

And she was gone, shuffling quickly to the nursery to check on the tiny gurgling sound that had whispered through the Baby Monitor. That was something, at least.

Shaking his head, James made sure to set his empty glass down on one of the sandstone coasters strategically placed around the redwood slab table before allowing himself to glare at his own son.

"You had yourself neutered? Jesus, Kev…"

"Not neutered, Dad," his son said. "I simply took responsibility for my own procreative future. Both 'Lyssa and I felt strongly about this. Why should the earth suffer just because we suddenly decided to succumb to a biological urge?"

James sat back into the chair's natural fiber cushions and tried to remember if he'd ever—in his entire life—thought of making love as simply a biological urge.

"And you don't care that your family name will die out with you?"

Kevin seemed to think about it for a moment.

Then shrugged.

"Not necessarily, no Besides," he said, winking, "Tiffers doesn't have to change her name when…and if she marries."

Tiffers. They should have bought a puppy. James rolled his eyes and was reaching for the pink and white gift bag on the table when his daughter-in-law breezed back in.

"Nothing to worry about," she announced as if both father and grandfather had been holding their breaths, waiting for their worse fears to be realized. "Tiff just did a little boomers."

Tiff.

"I brought something for the baby," James said, lifting the bag that had been so dutifully ooed and ahed over before being set down on the coffee table and promptly forgotten. "You might remember it, Kev."

"You didn't find all my original G.I. Joes, did you, Dad?" A new light came into his son's eyes as he took the bag—with its dancing teddy bears and matching bear rattle and bow—and began pawing through the layers of lavender tissue. "God, if you did they'll be worth a small fortu—Wow. Dad, I can't believe you found this."

"Omygod ..." M'Lyssa gasped, her hand dramatically stopping the flow of her caftan. "What IS it?"

James watched his son hold the almost completely bald toy up to his bug-eyed wife. And smiled. Secretly.

"It's Conan." Kevin said.

"What was Conan before he was hit by a car and killed," M'Lyssa asked.

Even James had to laugh at that one.

"No," Kevin said as he turned the toy around and ran his thumb nail over the scuffed black eyes. "Conan's my old teddy bear."

"That's a teddy bear?"

"A very ancient one," James said, pushing himself to his feet and feeling the room shift sluggishly to one side. As weak as the last drink was, it still had enough punch to make itself be felt. "As far as we can figure—it was Kevin's

Great Aunt Fiona who actually tried to trace down the history—it dates back to Fifth Century England."

His daughter-in-law's sneer straightened. Slightly.

"That old? I'm surprised it's still around. Are you sure you want to give it to us? I mean…shouldn't it be in a museum somewhere? Preferably in an air-tight container?"

James took a deep breath and immediately recognized his mistake when the room shifted to the other side—faster than it had the first time.

"It's a family tradition," he said, closing his eyes and waiting for the room to stop moving before continuing. "It goes to each baby of the family until a new one takes its place. And it looks like Tiffany's going to have it for quite a while…all things considering."

"You bombed, Dad?" his son asked. "Y'know, maybe you really should stay tonight. The futon's pretty darned comfortable and…"

"You're not saying we're supposed to put this…thing in Tiffany's crib, are you?" his daughter-in-law asked, effectively changing the subject before her husband finished doing something he would sorely regret. "Because if you are, then I'm sorry to say you're out of your mind."

James opened his eyes even though the room wasn't any more stable than it had been a moment earlier.

"You have to," he said softly. "It will protect her from the things that walk the night."

M'Lyssa stared and Kevin burst out laughing.

"God, Dad, you really are bombed. I remember when I was about seven or eight and I had that really bad nightmare…" He turned toward his wife, his fingers still kneading the toy's soft body. "I thought I saw something creeping around under my bed, y'know, monsters under the bed—every kid has them, and started screaming my bloody head off. Well, there comes good old Dad, looking worse than any monster I could make up, and tells me that as long as I have Conan nothing will ever happen to me.

"And nothing ever did happen to you, did it, Kev?" James asked. Until now, he wanted to add. "The…monsters under the bed never got you, did they?"

"Daddy Jim," M'Lyssa said, giving the ancient protector one last, disdainful look before settling herself into a straight back wicker chair. "The monsters under the bed never get any child."

The room shifted to the left and right (back and forth back and forth) as James walked toward his daughter-in-law.

"They got my little sister, Corliss," he said. "I—I didn't want to give her…Conan, so I snuck into her room when my mother and grandfather were asleep and took him back. She died that night. Because I took him away. He wasn't there to protect her from the monsters."

"Oh, Daddy Jim," his daughter-in-law twittered, "SIDS happens. Your sister's death didn't have anything to do with your taking back a toy. Children die…especially back when you were little. I'm just sorry you've been carrying around this guilt for so many years. Something like that really puts a strain on a person's aura."

Dear God. James exhaled slowly and looked over at his son. Who shrugged.

"Right. Will you humor an old man, at least, and put…the toy in with Tiffany?"

"Absolutely not," M'Lyssa hissed.

"Okay, maybe not next to her…maybe it'll still work if its just near her. How about sticking it at the far end of the crib?"

"No. Everything in that room has been sanitized and purified. I shouldn't even be allowing that…thing in the same house as Tiffany."

"'Lyssa, hang on a minute," Kevin said, getting to his feet, "let me handle this, okay? C'mon, Dad, I'll buy you a cup of coffee out in the kitchen, okay?"

His daughter-in-law was still grumbling while James followed his son out to the kitchen.

"Don't worry, about 'Lyssa," Kevin said, tucking the toy under one arm as he filled two mugs from the Mister Coffee. "She's just working through her New Mothering phase. In fact, she didn't even let the OB touch her until she watched him wash his surgical gloves. It's just hormones, Dad, don't take it personally."

James accepted the steaming mug and set it on the counter top without tasting it.

"I didn't, Kev...I never do...but you have to promise to put—Conan in Tiffany's crib. Please, Kevin...she's your child. The only child you'll ever have."

James saw a glimmer in his son's eyes.

"She'll kill me," Kevin said, setting his own untouched mug next to his father's and taking the toy out from under his arm.

"I don't think so."

"You don't know her...especially now that Tiff's here. I have to brush my teeth before I can even poke my head in to look at her. Bizarre."

"But what if I'm right about the monsters, Kev? Could you live with yourself knowing you could have saved your daughter but didn't?"

James reached out and touched the nubby head. Felt the warm fur and icy, cold pain he'd lived with since his sister died. "Please, Kevin...humor your poor old father. Please."

"I must be out of my mind," his son said, walking to the microwave mounted above the stove and popping open the smoked glass door. "But okay."

James felt the cold begin to lift until he saw his son toss Conan *neè* Cedric into the machine.

"What are you doing?"

"Killing germs," his son said, punching in some numbers. "You think three minutes on HIGH'll do it?"

James held his breath and prayed.

The unmistakable scent of cooked mutton filled the kitchen.

***

"Tiffers okay?" Kevin asked, still groggy from his wife's muttering departure twenty minutes earlier.

"I think we should re-evaluate our position on breast feeding,"'Lyssa said, making no effort to get back into the bed gently. "I mean you're missing all the fun."

Kevin tried to think of something supportive to say. And failed.

"Love you, babe," he said instead.

"Yeah. Oh, and you'll never guess what I found in Tiffany's bed while I was standing there being milked like a cow."

Oh oh. Kevin was suddenly awake.

"Uh, hon, I can explain…"

"Can you really?" The bed shook as she turned to face him. Even in the dark Kevin could see the anger etched into her face. "Can you really explain why you'd go against my specific wishes about exposing our day old child to an obviously —"

A low growl came from the tiny speaker in the Baby Monitor next to the bed.

"Shh, 'Lyssa, did you just hear that?"

"— diseased ridden piece of—"

The growl deepened…became a wet, undulating moan that

"'Lyssa…I'm serious…listen!"

"— antiquity that probably came—"

almost covered the sound of a baby waking into a bad dream.

Almost.

"— from some hovel somewhere and WHAT THE HELL ARE YOU D—"

Kevin clamped one hand over his wife's mouth and the other around the back of her neck—forced her to the mattress as he hissed again.

"Listen!"

There was no mistaking the sound coming through the monitor. His daughter's voice—thin and weak and screaming—rising above a sound Kevin remembered from his own childish nightmares; the soft, squishy sound of things creeping through the darkness under his bed …

…of monsters…

…back when there was nothing that could protect him except—

Kevin vaulted over his wife, ignoring her terrified sobbing as he raced down the hallway to the nursery…to the nursery with its white walls and rainbow mural and primary-colored furniture and Peter Rabbit Night-Lamp and Mother Goose Interactive Story Teller and post-natal monitoring devices and something that rose from the shadows beneath his daughter's tiny crib like a huge, clawed hand.

That was slowly descending.

M'Lyssa's scream shattered the ice that had formed around Kevin's soul and he fell forward onto his knees…a yard away from his daughter and the thing that was reaching down toward her. Kevin could see her tiny body convulsing beneath the fluffy white blanket…so little, so frightened …

…so alone.

He turned without getting up, grabbing his wife's arms and pulling her down to his level.

"WHERE'S CONAN?" he screamed over the piti-ful wailing of his dying child. "WHERE'D YOU PUT THE...BEAR?"

"I-I-I-"

His hand stung from where it made contact with the side of her face, but Kevin cocked his arm again—prepared to beat the answer out of her. If he needed to.

"I—I threw it away...it was so old, Kevin. OH MY GOD KEVIN WHAT IS IT? WHAT IS THAT WITH TIF-TIF-TIF—"

He left his wife in a huddled, screaming mass in the doorway of their daughter's room and careened off both sides of the narrow hallway, knocking down framed posters as he raced to the kitchen. The toy had to be in the garbage under the sink—it HAD to be—M'Lyssa didn't like to go out after dark...wouldn't have even to get back at him...wouldn't have...couldn't have...

Please, God, let it be there.

Kevin barely touched the already baby-proofed latch when the cabinet door exploded outward—shattering into a million pieces as something small and pale darted between his legs.

He turned just in time to see it disappear around the kitchen door, its claws making sparks against the no-wax flooring. Kevin hadn't gotten a good look at...it—just a brief glimpse, but the impression it left behind in his mind was one of a sinewy, hairless body and large, black eyes ...

...and a mouth that seemed to split the nubby head in half...a mouth filled with needle-sharp teeth...

A new sound filled the night, one that drowned out the sound of his wife and daughter's screams.

Kevin retraced his path down the hallway, taking

out the few remaining posters he'd missed the first time, and got to the nursery door just in time to see Conan ...

...Cedric...

...Old Bear...

...Oldie...

...and a hundred other names that whispered to him through the darkness...

—to watch the ancient Protector stand over his newborn daughter and raise one skeletal thin paw toward the descending shadow; heard the guttural hiss and saw the shadow fade until it was nothing more than the soft, empty darkness beneath his child's crib.

Nothing more.

"Ke-Kevin?"

He helped his wife to her feet, allowing her to lean on him as they walked to the crib. And peeked in.

Tiffany was sound asleep, her lips making kissing sounds as they nursed an imaginary breast...one tiny hand poking out from beneath the blanket, chubby fingers clutching one of the few remaining patches of reddish brown fur.

"Kev? Did something just happen? Wh-what are we doing here?"

Kevin hugged his wife close and smiled down at their sleeping baby.

"We just wanted to look in on her, don't you remember?"

"Oh, oh yeah. I guess. Kevin, do you really think we should let her keep that...thing? I mean, it really doesn't look all that good."

"He looks fine. Good, old bear," Kevin whispered, tucking the blanket in around his threadbare sides—tracing the outline of an embroidered heart on the bald belly the way he used to. When he was little. "Thank you."

"Well, okay, I guess. But what do you think we

should call him? I don't think Conan's a very good name for a little girl's teddy bear, do you?"

Kevin cocked his head to one side, listening.

"Faith," he said softly. "This time her name's Faith."

TOMB WITH A VIEW

From his office/living quarters sixty-two stories up, Murray Feinstein watched the noxious brown-gray cloud as it ebbed and flowed its way down West Sixty-seventh, lapping against the crumbling facades of what used to be trendy galleries and Indo-Texan eateries, curling into the narrow gullies between the high-rises, sneaking like a cat-burglar through broken windows, rolling undisturbed toward the great emptiness that once was Central Park.

Sighing, he leaned forward until he could see the top of the deserted office building across the street, then counted down.

…fifty-four…fifty-three…fifty-two and a half…

It was up another half-story since yesterday.

(Good-bye, Casa de Ngo, Sullivan's Ol'Timer Boozeria. Don't forget to write, Steve and Edie's All-night Escort Service. Ciao.)

His breath fogged the glass around his face and he quickly wiped it away. At this rate, he'd have to start thinking about moving again soon.

"Moving up in the world." He chuckled softly. "Maybe even see what the penthouse is like. So who would know?"

Even as he contemplated it, he dismissed the possibility. At least for now. Moving into the penthouse would have to come later, when the growing smog bank finally swallowed the city. Then he could either try strapping on portable oxygen tanks and walking down all ninety-five stories, or he could light up a stogie and do a belly flop into eternity.

"Probably be dead before I hit, anyway," he muttered, just to hear something besides the steady hum of the Maxi-Plus air-purification unit next to him, guaranteed or your money back. "No breathable air past the twenty-seventh floor."

Murray shrugged. The thought of death really didn't bother him anymore. After all, he was a seventh-generation New Yorker. Death loomed at every street corner, so why let it worry you? The only thing that overshadowed his contemplation was the obvious lack of an audience.

Once, a dive from the penthouse of the Koch Memorial Towers would have made the headlines throughout the five boroughs. Now he'd be lucky if the computerized National Guard Surveillance street-sweepers could manage to slurp up all the pieces.

And no one would even see that. He'd be unceremoniously ejected into the East River Land Fill with the rest of the day's garbage. No tears, no muss, no fuss. They probably thought he was dead already.

Murray caught his reflection looking back at him, and shook his head.

"So what are you looking at, Mr. This-Is-My-Home-and-I'm-Staying-Right-Here?" he asked the rotund little man with glasses. "That's right, you! You stand there looking like maybe all your friends had the right idea."

His reflection stared back silently.

"Go live in Kansas, you asked them, the Kansas with the tornadoes and pollen so bad each spring you can't breath there either? So what do the experts know anyway, you told the Hammners. So what if the city's grown so much there's no more natural ventilation? You think the president's gonna let the greatest city in the world die for a little ventilation? No! No, any day now they'll send enough money to fix things, just you watch."

The little man in the reflection pulled nervously at the synthetic nylon body suit.

"So what happens? So the president calls a news conference from his summer home in Cuba and tells everybody to leave New York. Get out, he tells them, and don't come back for a hundred years, maybe longer. And everybody starts packing. So what do you do, Mr. I-Know-Better-Than-the-President? Do you take the fortune your family made by supporting kosher meals to the lunar bases and follow them? No! No, you call in your own experts and spend a fortune building air-purifiers. And what happens? Everyone leaves town faster.

"So now what? Now you got your purifiers in half the buildings in Manhattan, running from a generator you bought because Con Ed went bankrupt, talking to yourself because everyone's in Kansas, waiting for the next tornado or dust storm."

His reflection couldn't answer that one.

Nodding, Murray directed his attention downward to the almost-obscured mauve-and-gold GRAND RE-OPENING banner across the street. Wong's Old-fashioned Vietnamese Hot Dog Emporium was gone—devoured sometime in the night along with its artificially sweetened sauerkraut and dog-meat chili.

Old Man Wong…When the smog closed his ground-floor eatery, he'd moved up to the third floor. A week later, his hand-painted banner had drooped listlessly from a window on the sixteenth. By the time he reached the twentieth, the old man had somehow acquired a sizable piece of canvas and eye-numbing paint and had produced the now-familiar masterpiece of defiance.

He'd made it to the forty-fifth floor when the rats finally caught up with him.

Murray had been two stories farther up, just getting settled into his own new surroundings, when he heard the first screams. He'd left the exterior audio on as he usually did—"Force of habit," he told himself. At first he thought a police car or some other public-service siren had mistakenly entered the concrete canyons and was, at the moment, choking to death.

By the time Murray set down the plastic box he'd carried up since the third floor and walked to the window, he was just in time to see the old man, rats the size of poodles hanging on to his arms and legs, crash through the double-strength floor-to-ceiling picture window.

Despite the lunge outward, Wong's right hand had somehow managed to catch hold of the banner and hang on. He hung there for fifteen minutes while one of the larger rats worked on his wrist, and Murray watched all of it. There wasn't anything else to watch since the BBC station in Jersey had stopped transmitting.

Wong fell without another sound and Murray had watched his red-tinted fall until he hit the main smog bank and disappeared from view.

It took another four days before the hand released its grip and followed, and by then the smog was only ten stories down.

Murray felt another sigh building at the back of his throat and quickly swallowed it.

"No," he snorted angrily. "Murray Feinstein ain't finished either."

He patted the air-purifier confidently just as something thudded against the walled-over and reinforced central-heating duct.

"What, you think I want your company? I got enough troubles already, thank you."

Sure, as if the rats weren't enough, now he had cockroaches to contend with. Ah, what the hell, he thought, waving at the kevlar-reinforced covering on the air ducts, New York's always had bugs and rats. So what else is new?

Just like smog, right, Murray?

At first the smog wasn't so bad. After all, hadn't it finally cleared the streets of drug-runners, muggers, street gangs, and political canvassers? So what if the rats and roaches proved smarter than their human counterparts? So what if the only living things interested in your cockamamy air-conditioning are looking at you as a blue-plate special? So what's so different?

His neighbor scratched again, thumped twice, and was silent, obviously taking the hint that there'd be no free lunch today. Smiling, he threw his reflection a wink and headed for the room's self-contained food processor. One other benefit of living in a post-1990s Sky-riser—the best syntho-soy products going.

Patting his convex waistline, Murray dialed up the picture of chicken soup and flipped the switch.

The whole process took fifty seconds; Murray timed it on the old-fashioned pocket watch he carried on a chain around his neck, pockets having gone the way of neck-ties and environmental initiatives. Twenty-two seconds longer than breakfast.

When it arrived it was cold, but only had a half-dozen rat hairs and roach antennae floating in it, so that was something, at least.

Murray set a place for himself on the Real Wood (copyright, 1997) desk and skimmed his soup with the plastic spoon the syntho had included.

"Immigrants," he shouted to his reflection as he

wiped the spoon off on one of the sheets of rice paper that lay scattered in front of him. "That's what we need. Give this town a real shot in the arm."

He nodded, took a slurp, grimaced, and put the spoon down.

"Just like before. Thousands of immigrants pouring in every day, bringing their energy, their yearnings to be free"—Murray glanced past his reflection to the giant marvels of concrete and steel beyond the glass—"their money."

So who would tell them that he, Murray Feinstein didn't own every building in the city? Who would complain? Not the real owners. If they'd cared enough for their property and city, they would never have left it for Kansas, may they all sit on haystacks and get needles in their hemorrhoids.

Slapping the table and ignoring the fact that he'd showered the expensive desk with coagulating chicken soup, Murray stood up and held his arms out to the silent city.

"We're gonna make it, kids. Just let your old Uncle Murray handle it. Somewhere on this dirty little planet there are people who are willing to put up with a little inconvenience for the sake of living in New York, and I'm going to find them."

His reflection seemed to fade the more he spoke, blending into the background of silver and gray until it was no longer perceptible.

"Yes, sir, yes, sir—that's just what I'm gonna do."

***

Murray started his Urban Replenishment Campaign the next morning at sunrise, when he hooked up the portable CB he had picked up on nineteen to the building's antiquated public-address system. Back at the turn of the century, he'd heard, building managers used to talk back and forth across the city on these things.

It would have been like listening to giants, he thought and felt a shiver course its way down his spine.

"Will be again," he promised, wheezing toward the normal gray-green skyline. The smog level ninety-five stories up was still tolerable, thank God! "We're going to have people again —talking, laughing…spending money."

Murray keyed the automatic cassette loop on the transmitter and leaned back against the naked metal tower, resting while his recorded voice echoed across the city.

"Bring me your strong, your healthy, your rugged individuals longing for the joy of conquest! Come join the adventure. New York has never been a better investment for the self-starter. Sky-risers awaiting occupancy. Unlimited space. Live high and free above the clouds. Contact: Murray Feinstein, concierge, Koch Memorial Towers. Be one of the few. The proud. The brave!"

Murray listened to it for an hour while he got his strength back, smiling each time it ran. He would let it play throughout the four full hours of daylight, he decided as he set the automatic timer. Better exposure that way. Besides, he didn't know anyone anymore who didn't have to take a whole handful of things to help them through the twenty hours of darkness. Advertising at night would be a waste of good generator power.

Satisfied at last that his message would be heard, and with dreams of a nifty little sideline marketing "I -heart-NOx" novelties dancing round his head, Murray pushed himself to his feet and walked toward the top of the covered stairwell.

He was halfway across the asphalt roofing when the small amber light over the elevator door blinked on, indication of a car coming up.

Coming up? Couldn't be! The elevators went out fifteen months ago, when the caustic smog that filled the basement finally ate its way through to the control panel. Murray could only guess what had happened to the building's super—a skinny kid with pimples who slept on a cot next to the panel board.

Murray stared at the light and rubbed his eyes. Keeping his hand over his face, he took as deep a breath as he could without choking, and counted to ten. Must be seeing things, boychik, he chided himself. Been living alone so long you came down with mental diarrhea. One more minute and your brains'll come pouring out your ears.

He took another breath, coughed, and opened his eyes.

The light was still on and now he could feel the all-but-forgotten vibration through the padded soles of his shoes.

Maybe the pimple-faced kid had gotten away, finally got the damn elevator running. Murray smiled at the thought of being able to ride back down to his cubbyhole in mechanical comfort—watching the softly tinted floor indicators wink on and off seductively, listening to the rats squeal as the plastic and steel box slipped upward...

...listening to the rats...

A new image etched itself on the insides of his eyeballs.

Maybe the car was filled with rats. And him, like the rest of the poor schmucks who hadn't had enough sense to get out of the smog when the getting was good, just standing there like the world's biggest kosher dinner. Yessiree, ladies and rodents, right this way for Chez Murray's Rooftop Dining, kosher cuisine at its finest.

He'd be lucky if he made it to the stairs before they ate his legs off.

Murray held his breath and slowly began walking

backwards away from the double-wide door, convinced that if he took his eyes away for one moment it would open and spew out a lethal, wriggling cargo.

"So why are we tippy-toeing, Mr. I'm-Going-to-Make-Millions?" he asked himself, still backing away. "Think your newfound wealth's going to make any difference now? Fat lot of good money's going to make when you're racing man-killing rodents down thirty-three flights of stairs. You think maybe you can offer them a bribe not to eat you?"

He was less than a yard from the stairwell when the emergency phone next to the elevator door buzzed to life.

"Now that's something I never heard rats do before," he shouted.

Behind him, the transmitter went into its prerecorded spiel. "Bring me your strong, your healthy, your rugged individuals ..."

Sure, why not? Maybe his message was getting through already.

Smiling, smoothing down what little hair remained on his head, Murray walked back to the elevator and lifted the clear plastic phone to his lips.

"Murray Feinstein here. May I help you?"

The voice on the other end was hollow-sounding, the words echoing slightly, as if the caller were at the bottom of an abandoned well. Naturally.

"You have...rooms for...rent?"

Murray felt the blood surge through his veins. It was an odd sensation, as if he'd been dead all these long months and never known it. He shook the thought out of his head and tried to suck in his stomach, without much success.

"Have I got rooms? Rooms of every size and shape. You name it, Murray Feinstein's got it."

There was a momentary silence on the line while,

Murray presumed, the voice thought it over; then ...

"Good. We'll be...right up ..."

Murray tossed the phone back into its molded cradle and did one of the only two dance steps he knew. "We," the voice had said, "WE."

"Hear that, New York?" he shouted to the columns of rock and steel. "We got customers! Gonna be great again, just you wait. Won't be any time before we can snap our fingers at them Kansas Cowboys."

To emphasize his words, Murray snapped his fingers just as the elevator doors slid open.

There must have been two dozen of them crammed into a space designed to hold no more than ten. Each wore a crude breathing apparatus over the head, attached to a bulbous air sack that expanded and contracted with each breath, like some kind of external lung. The image turned Murray's stomach slightly, but he managed to keep his smile in place.

Their ragged clothing, which appeared to be made from torn upholstery and curtain material, was so bulky and ill-fitting that Murray couldn't tell which were male and female—or even whether there were mixed genders in the group. Not wishing to offend and thereby blow the whole deal, Murray bowed majestically from the waist, his right hand sweeping backwards in a large arc.

There was a muffled twitter from one of the smaller bundles in the crowd.

"Welcome, my friends," he began, as if he'd been saying it all his life. "Welcome to the Ko—to Feinstein's Golden Towers. I am Murray Feinstein, your amiable host." He bowed again, less dramatically.

They filed out of the car en masse, as if they were afraid to move independently; Murray backed up accordingly. As weak as the timid midday sun was, they seemed to shy away from it, preferring to stay in the shadows.

Murray forced another inch of smile to his lips. "Air's fine up here," he said, tapping his chest and pretending to take a deep breath. "Only about a sixty percent pollution rate today. Go ahead and take off your...equipment, it's fresh as a day in spring."

The group shifted uneasily for a moment, but no one made a move toward their heavy face masks. Finally a taller member walked to the front of the group and extended a gloved hand. Murray took it without reservation and pumped enthusiastically.

The hand under the glove felt thin and bony.

"How many...rooms do you have, Mr. Feinstein?" asked the same voice he had spoken to earlier.

"How many you need?" Murray countered, letting go of the man's hand and pirouetting in place. Another twitter from the crowd. "I got rights to all the property west of the landfill."

The man nodded and Murray could almost make out the features behind the thick glass. Almost. But not quite. And if the eyes that stared out at him were any indication of the face, Murray was just as glad the man had decided to keep the gear on.

They reminded him of rat's eyes—but not as pleasant.

"We have over...a thousand...in our...group."

"A th-thousand?" Not much for a city that once hosted nine million, but a decent start. Pulling himself up to his full size, another quarter of an inch, Murray leveled what he liked to think of as his "snake charmer's" eye at the man's faceplate and raised one eyebrow. "You got money?" he asked. "New York's mine, but I ain't giving it away."

The group shifted again and the man standing in front of Murray turned to receive a stained gunnysack, then upended it at Murray's feet.

Thick rolls of multicolored New York currency bounced amid tangles of gold and gems.

Swallowing the drool that suddenly filled his mouth, Murray nodded as casually as he could.

"Nice, nice. I assume it's all yours?"

The man cocked his head behind the thick mask. "It is...now," came the muffled reply.

Bending quickly, Murray swept the fortune back into its sack and stood up. "That's fine. Now, how about we start with this building and work our way out? That sound okay?" He hugged the heavy bag to his chest like a precious child. "I have some wonderful suites down on sixty-two— that's my floor, but anything up to the penthouse will be perfectly all right."

The group seemed to draw back into itself, and Murray sank his fingers deeper into the filthy material.

"I—I mean, of course any building would be all right. Any one at all..."

The group inched back toward the elevator. The bitter taste of a deal falling through filled Murray's mouth.

"And—and you can have, you can have your choice of floors. Any floor at all!"

The group stopped.

"Any floor...Mr. Feinstein?" the spokesman asked.

The smile, forced as it was, bloomed again. "Of course. Should I tell you where to live? Not me, not Murray Feinstein. You live on any floor you want."

Muffled sounds of contentment filtered through the heavy breathing bags. Murray felt his fingers release their death grip on the booty sack.

"Thank you...Mr. Feinstein," the spokesman said. "We will start with the bottom floors...and work our way...up."

Murray felt his jaw unhinge. "Bu—but..." Careful, he reminded himself, you almost blew the deal once already. "Won't it be a little...well, hard to breathe down there?"

Another mutter passed through the crowd, but this time it sounded like laughter.

"We're...used to it...Mr. Feinstein." The man took a step forward and Murray felt a shiver go up his spine. "We've been...living with...pollution for...generations now."

"I—I don't understand," Murray said.

The man took another step and gently caressed his face mask.

"Carbon monoxide is...our life's breath. Because our...forefathers chose to...dwell...below your streets, Mr. Feinstein, we survived this...catastrophe."

This time Murray was sure he heard laughter coming from the group.

"When your...kind fled the city...they left...most of their valuables behind." Murray could see the faintest hint of a smile behind the glass. "We have...claimed them as...you've claimed...this city."

Murray hadn't even realized he had continued to back up until his spine struck the side of the covered stairwell. The gunnysack fell almost noiselessly from his hands.

"We're not going...to harm you...Mr. Feinstein. We have our honor," the man said, bending down to retrieve the bag and then thrusting it into Murray's slack grasp. "We simply...want a more...comfortable life. And since...you are the local...real estate agent ..."

The man let his voice drop into silence. So, Murray heard himself ask, what are you going to do now, Mr. Smarty-Pockets? Rent rooms to mutant smog-suckers who steal from the dead? Turn New York into a walking graveyard? Strap on your own air tanks for a weekly game of pinochle with a bunch of exhaust zombies? Are you that greedy, Murray Feinstein?

"Of course," he said, slinging the bag over his shoulder. "Now, how about a nice two-bed-and bath, over-looking Central Park?"

UNDER THE HAYSTACK

Little boy blue, come blow your horn,
the sheep's in the meadow
the cow's in the corn.
But where is the boy who looks after the sheep?
He's under the haystack
fast asleep.

The nursery rhyme was printed in medium blue ink next to the picture of a tiny boy half buried beneath a golden mountain of hay, repeating itself two-hundred and six times across the north wall, fifty three times (because of the door and built-in closet) across the east wall, and one-hundred and three (forced air heating duct) across the south wall.

Three-hundred sixty two little boys under the haystack fast asleep.

Maggie had counted them every day since putting the paper up. Every day since the amniocentesis had determined that the baby growing inside her was alive and healthy and male. A little boy blue sleeping under her heart.

A little blue boy.

Sleeping.

Forever.

Maggie tightened her grip on the smooth wood armrests and slowly pushed herself out of the antique rocker Sean had found at an estate sale. It was getting harder to move. Just like the doctor had said it would.

"Your body has already begun shutting down certain…systems. Preparing itself. Imagine it similar to your monthly cycle. In fact it's actually very similar. The only difference in this case is that the non-viable tissue the uterus is discharging is the—"

No.

Maggie held her breath until she got to the floor-to-ceiling bay window that made up the entire west facing wall.

It had been the window that ultimately ended their house hunting sojourns into the wilds of suburbia.

The room was small and narrow, barely thirteen feet by nine, but the window more than made up for the overall lack of space. It opened the room to the sun and sky and stars. Maggie had always wanted a bay window of her own—something she could curl into on rainy days or stretch out in on sunny ones. But this window was for her little boy blue. This window would be the glass prow of the Fairy boat that would sail him to dreamland each night and return him safely each morning.

Would have been.

Maggie let her hands cup the smooth roundness of her belly when she reached the crib. Plain white oak. Midnight blue bumpers and ruffle. No pillow. The comforter pale blue, it's central design coordinated to match the wallpaper. Little Boy Blue under an embroidered haystack. Fast asleep.

Forever.

"Wake up," Maggie whispered to the silent bulge under her fingers. "Please wake up."

But this little boy blue couldn't any more than the others could.

"Sometimes these things just happen, Maggie. It

wasn't your fault." The doctor's voice again…calm and
unemotional as he pointed to the fuzzy white-on-gray
UltraSound pictures and confirmed what Maggie already
knew. That her little boy blue had fallen fast asleep and
would never wake up again.

I'm sorry.

Maggie's hands slid further down the curve of her
belly. The baby had always been so active. Always. Moving,
squirming, arms and feet poking her as he tried to get comfortable. Nights were the worst.

Maggie couldn't so much as set a paperback on top
of her belly without sudden and velvet soft retaliation. Sean
loved that. He'd turn onto his side and watch whatever book
she was trying to read jerk and jiggle. It convinced him that
their son would grow up to be either a publisher or the
bouncer at a Country Western Bar.

When he grew up.

But wouldn't.

Because sometimes these things happen and it was-
n't her fault.

I'm sorry.

No longer needing to be careful of her swollen
belly or the fragile life it once carried, Maggie leaned into
the white pine slats and traced the comforter's embroidered
design with the tip of her finger.

Little boy blue.

She'd known something was wrong all afternoon of
that last day. But didn't do anything about it.

I'm sorry.

He "woke up" earlier than usual, just before dawn,
his tiny fists and feet pounding against the inside of her
womb as if he were trying to punch his way out.

I'm sorry.

It'd been so intense that going back to sleep was

impossible. Sean even laughed when he finally came down-stairs to find her leaning backwards against the kitchen sink, a half-filled tumbler of orange juice doing the Cha-cha-cha against the top of her belly.

"Linebacker," Sean said before going to work, speaking directly to the quivering front of her maternity smock as if she wasn't there—a private joke between father and son. "Or maybe a running back. Either one."

When he grew up.

Big joke.

Because all morning the baby had kicked and squirmed and wiggled. Old Wiggle-butt, Maggie's pet name for him now, David Andrew or Nicholas James when he was born. Dave or Nicky. Nicky or Dave. But that was for later, after he was born. That last day Old Wiggle-butt suited him best.

Until just after noon.

When he stopped wiggling (I'm sorry) so suddenly that Maggie had actually caught her breath. She'd spent the rest of the afternoon tip-toeing around the house pretending he was just sleeping…that—any minute now—he'd wake up and jab her with his foot or elbow. Any minute. Now. To let her know he was all right.

She was crying when Sean got home from work.

Hysterical by the time they drove to the hospital.

Silent when she lay on the cold, paper draped examining table and stared at the UltraSound picture.

Sometimes these things happen.

It's not your fault.

"I'm sorry," Maggie said out loud and closed her eyes. The wallpapered room and the crib and the window and the dreams of things that would never happen disap-peared.

Everything disappeared.

But him. Her little boy blue deep inside her.

Heavy. Unmoving.

A dead weight.

under the haystack, fast asleep

Maggie opened her eyes and looked down into a backyard that was twice as big as their entire apartment back in the city. A magpie was hip-hopping in front of the early autumn chrysanthemum hedge and there was a fat squirrel running laps across the back fence.

She moved her hands away from the unmoving bulge at her waist and curled her fingers around the crib's side-railing. It was a wonderful backyard—big enough for the swing sets and tree houses and sand boxes that would never be needed.

After they found out about the baby, Sean had started talking about building a deck. Maybe even a gazebo, how about that? You always wanted a gazebo, didn't you Maggie?

Maggie couldn't remember.

Taking a deep breath, she felt the air claw its way past the tightness in her throat.

They were going to take the baby in the morning; induce labor three months early then autopsy the tiny blue thing that came out of her body to make sure it wasn't her fault.

The doctor had patted her hand and smiled when he explained the procedure—a saline solution would be introduced into her womb and her body would expel the "material" in three to five hours.

Tomorrow morning.

Tomorrow morning she would go into labor and give birth. Tomorrow night they would release her from the hospital and she'd come home.

Alone.

There would be no hurried calls to parents or friends stopping by to coo and sigh at the nursery's Visitor's Window. There'd be no flowers or "It's a Boy!" balloons or holding the baby so gently as Sean wheeled her to the car.

Tomorrow there'd be nothing in her hands or womb.

Tomorrow she'd go home empty.

"No," she told the Magpie, because no one—not Sean or the doctors or her parents or their friends—had heard her the hundred of other times she said it, "I don't want to."

"But I thought you were looking forward to going with me," a familiar voice said from the doorway.

Maggie was trying to blink back the tears as she turned around, but not fast enough to keep Sean from noticing.

"Oh, babe." He came to her quickly, his running shoes thumping across the thick carpet (so the baby wouldn't hurt himself when he began walking and took a tumble oh god), long arms reaching out to pull her in. "I wish you wouldn't keep doing this to yourself. You know what the doctor said."

Sometimes these things happen…it's not your fault.

Maggie nodded against the warm flannel covering his shoulder, letting the material soak the tears away.

"I know," she whispered and felt him sigh, his chest rising and falling effortlessly. No hitch. No sob. Nothing.

This wasn't the first time he'd found her crying next to the empty crib. But it would be the last. Maggie lifted her head just enough to see over his shoulder and bit the inside of her cheek until she tasted blood.

"I think it might be better if I did what Dr. Melton suggested," Sean said. "Just put these things into storage until…we need them. He said we could start again in six months. Once you're…you know."

What? Maggie wanted to ask. Healed?

But she didn't. She nodded and sidestepped along the crib, hugging herself so he couldn't; watching the sunlight ignite the blond-red hair and bright blue eyes she'd playfully ordered the baby to inherit over her own mouse-brown hair and hazel eyes.

A lifetime ago.

"I'm sorry," she said.

Sean gave her a crooked smile, then took her hand and gently pulled her toward the door.

"Not to worry about it, kid. I think you'll feel better once this stuff is packed away. Out of sight sort of thing…you know. I'll start on this tomorrow when you're …" Maggie felt his fingers tighten for an instant. "Sure you don't want to go with me today? I really would like some company on this trip. You know how awful my taste is sometimes."

Liar.

Sean's taste was wonderful—his eye for value remarkable. Which was probably the reason "their" Antique/Collectable business drew more than just browsers and Lookie-loos. He needed her to help him go through an estate sale looking for bargains like he needed a third eye, but if she said no he'd probably find some reason for not going. Stay home to keep the two eyes he did have locked on her.

"Okay," Maggie said when they got to the hallway. "Sounds like fun."

Liar.

"Great! And you'll see, once we're up into the high country and start driving through all that gorgeous autumn color you're going to feel a hundred percent better."

Maggie smiled. Nodded. And just managed to stop herself from screaming when Sean closed the door.

***

It was beautiful in the high country.

And Maggie hated herself for noticing.

With the first hint of winter already in the air, the aspen and cottonwood had begun their yearly dance of death; the mountain sides a patchwork of lemon yellow, gold, orange and flame, amid the constant backdrop of Blue Spruce and green pine. Breathtaking, God dammit.

"What was the name of that turn off?" Sean said, tapping the opened Classified section that lay across her legs (not her lap…because she didn't have one…not yet…tomorrow). "Skylark Lane or Skywood?"

Maggie squinted at the address circled in red, desperately trying to keep the paper steady despite the Trooper's bump-and-grind, kidney-busting suspension.

God, why did she have to think about kidneys busting?

Since the beginning of her fourth month her kidneys had felt as if they'd shrunken to the size of walnuts. All she had to do was look at a glass of water and feel that all too urgent twinge. Even with the baby dea…Even now.

Maggie licked her lips and pressed her knees together.

"Something the matter, babe?" Sean asked, steering with only the fingers of his left hand as he patted her thigh with his right.

He'd stopped using her name when they found out about the baby, substituting babe or honey or sweetheart or something equally as safe and non-threatening. Tomorrow he'd call her Maggie again.

When he brought her back from the hospital.

Empty.

"Hon?"

Maggie squirmed in the bucket seat, crossed one leg over the other. It didn't help.

"Think we can find a rest stop anywhere up here?" She puffed out her cheeks. "I guess I shouldn't have had that glass of orange juice before we left the house."

Sean grimaced and instantly began scanning the narrow two-lane road ahead. Maggie could see the reflection of aspen and cottonwood in his sunglasses. Their colors looked dead, tinted blue.

"God, babe, I don't know what to tell you. There doesn't seem to be anything around."

Maggie nodded, accepting, and turned toward the side window just in time to see a rutted dirt road appear between two towering pines. A bright blue street sign gleamed in the afternoon sun, a red-and-white cardboard ESTATE SALE sign had been taped to the pole. A narrow black arrow pointed straight up.

"THERE!" The seat belt cut into her swollen belly when Sean hit the brakes. Maggie let it.

"WHAT?"

Maggie pointed to the signs and quickly verified the street name against the circled ad. "Skywood Lane. This is the right place." Maggie leaned forward over the paper, letting the restraint cut deeper as she tried to follow the road through the trees. "I think."

Sean had pulled off his glasses and exhaled loudly.

"Geeze, I wish you'd have given me a little more warning. Hon. I don't want to drop the transmission this far out in the boonies."

"Sorry."

"I thought we were about to hit a deer or some-thing."

"I said I was sorry."

He kept looking at her, his eyes deepening to gray.

Maggie tried crossing her legs in the opposite direction. That didn't help either.

"You okay?"

No, Maggie wanted to scream, I'm NOT okay! My baby's dead. My little boy blue will never wake up and tomorrow they're going to take him out of me and cut him up. I'm not okay. I'll NEVER be okay again!

"Just have to go to the bathroom," she muttered. "Maybe I can use the one at the house. If we ever find it."

That ended the staring contest.

Nodding, Sean slipped the glasses back over his eyes and turned the Trooper onto the narrow washboard road. He was angry, Maggie could tell by his silence and the grim line his lips formed, but that was all right because she was angry, too.

She just wished they had been angry about the same thing.

***

Sean saw the house first—another cardboard ESTATE SALE sign nailed to the front of a split-rail fence— and instantly began muttering breathlessly about the size and apparent age of the place, appraising antiques he hadn't yet seen, and mentally adding a "reasonable" mark up to the treasures he was undoubtedly going to find.

Maggie didn't say anything.

She used to. Once. A long time ago, she thought. Back when traveling the highways and back roads looking for antiques and "collectibles" had been fun. Back when there had just been the two of them.

Maggie uncrossed her legs and stared straight ahead as Sean pulled up next to a dusty white Plymouth.

There was still just the two of them.

"Here we are, honey," Sean said, opening his door. "Hang tight and I'll help you out."

"I can manage," Maggie said, more quickly than she'd intended. "You just go find out if there's a bathroom I can use. If not…ask where I can find a friendly tree."

She thought she heard him laugh as he jogged toward the house, but didn't care if he had or not. The pain in her bladder and weight of her dead baby had become the center of her world; beyond that nothing mattered.

Nothing.

Her legs felt like lead as she got out of the car and began following the path he'd taken. Each step sent shivering vibrations through her aching bladder.

"Hon? It's okay." Maggie looked at the birdlike, gray haired woman standing at her husband's side and smiled weakly.

"This is very kind of you," she said as Sean took her hand and helped her into the house like she was some kind of invalid. "I'm really very embarrassed—"

"Oh, honey, there's nothing to be embarrassed about," the old woman said, stepping out of the way. "Bathroom's just down the hall to the left."

"Maggie," she heard Sean say over her shoulder, "this is Mrs. Jenkins."

"Oh, good heavens, there's time enough for introductions later, this poor girl's in a hurry. Believe me, I know. Not that I ever had any little ones myself, never did get a chance to marry or…But I had a lot of friends who had children and when they got as big as you they couldn't go for more than fifteen minutes before having to find a necessary."

The old woman stopped talking just long enough to lean back on the heels of her worn sneakers and gaze down at Maggie's belly.

"Let's see, you must be about —"

Sean stepped between Maggie and the old woman and gave her a gently shove. Protecting her. From the kindness of strangers.

"You go ahead, hon. I'll talk to Mrs. Jenkins."

Maggie didn't stop moving until she reached the peach-and-white bathroom and closed (locked) the door behind her. Suddenly exhausted, she leaned against the door jam and took a deep breath. The room smelled faintly of bleach and baby powder-scented air freshener.

Just like all the ESTATE SALE houses she and Sean had visited over the year. Part of her wondered if some company somewhere was marketing an air freshener designed especially to mask the scent of death.

She'd have to look into that.

Tomorrow.

Pushing away from the door, Maggie turned on both the hot and cold water taps before turning her attentions to the necessary—an almond colored commode almost completely hidden by a orange fur lid and seat cover. She'd turned on the water not because she thought they might hear her, but because she could hear them.

"...lost the baby..."

"...horrible, I'm so sorry..."

"...says we can have another...not her fault ..."

"...sometimes these things happen for the best..."

"...just went to sleep..."

Under the haystack.

***

"Ah, there you are."

The gray haired woman, Mrs. Jenkins, was waiting for Maggie in the living room, a tall glass of water in her hand.

"I thought you might be thirsty, I remember my friends…" The old woman smiled suddenly. "When I first moved up here I was thirsty all the time."

Maggie said a muffled "Thank you" as she took the glass and found, much to her amazement, that she really was thirsty. Half the glass disappeared before she had to take a breath.

"I'm so sorry about running off at the mouth like that, dear," the old woman said, directing Maggie to an over-stuffed wing chair before lowering herself to the arm of the mismatched couch opposite. "It has to be the hardest thing to lose a baby."

But I haven't lost him. They're going to TAKE him from me! It took the rest of the water to force the words down.

"My you were thirsty. Would you like another?"

"No. Thank you. You've been so kind already, but I really should go and…and find my…"

my little boy blue is fast asleep and he won't wake up. He'll never wake up again.

Never.

Maggie wasn't even aware she was crying until the old woman left her perch and wrapped rail-thin arms around her shoulders. "I-I-I'm sorry," Maggie sobbed, frantically wiping her eyes off on the sleeve of her smock. If Sean saw her like this, he might make her go into the hospital tonight. "I don't…it's the …" She swallowed. "I really should find my husband."

"You just settle down and don't worry about that husband of yours." Mrs. Jenkins laughed and Maggie heard its echo through her cheek. "Last time I saw him he was in Seventh Heaven up in Albert's study…knee deep in dusty old books and smiling like a little boy on Christmas morn-ing. Oh, God…I'm sorry."

Maggie nodded and sniffed back another sob. Leaning back, she broke the old woman's grip and forced herself to smile. At least her lips felt like they were smiling.

"Sean does love books," she said. "Was Albert your husband?"

The laughter, minus the echo, answered her. "Lord no, Albert was my older brother. I came to live with him just after his wife died, let's see…that must have been, oh…thirty, thirty-five years ago this winter."

Maggie watched the old woman walk back to the couch and hover nervously next to the arm. She doesn't want to sit, Maggie thought, in case I break down again.

"That was nice of you," she said, smoothing the smock down over her belly. "Not many sisters would be willing to live with their brothers, let alone take care of them for that long. I know I wouldn't."

One of Mrs. Jenkins' knees crackled when she finally gave in to gravity and age and sat back down. Maggie could almost hear her mental sigh of relief.

"Oh, don't get me wrong…I'm no Mother Teresa and never have been. I wanted a family, children…sorry… but I didn't have a choice." Mrs. Jenkins pressed her hands into the small of her back and leaned backward to another series of snaps and pops. "Albert and I were twins and I sort of felt obligated. He took Jenny's death real hard…maybe a little bit too hard if you catch my meaning."

When Maggie shook her head, the old woman twirled her right index finger in a circle against her temple and momentarily crossed her eyes.

"That's why I'm having this 'Estate Sale' so soon after his funeral…I want to get rid of all that craziness about Jenny and the baby as soon as possible and get on with the rest of my life."

Maggie felt her hands fold themselves around her motionless belly.

"They had a baby?"

Mrs. Jenkins' forehead refolded itself along the crease lines when she frowned.

"Lord, I should be shot. I am so sorry. Your husband told me about your…troubles and here I am running off about my crazy brother."

"No, please, it's all right. Tell me."

Mrs. Jenkins' sigh was lost in a sudden thump-thump-crash from directly overhead.

"Oops, someone must have found that old bowling ball I was always tripping over. Man never did know when to throw anything ou…"

"Please, Mrs. Jenkins," Maggie said, holding her stomach so tight the muscles were beginning to tremble. "Tell me about the baby."

Another sigh, this one audible, filled the still air between them. Out of the corner of her eye, Maggie saw a bearded man with glasses duck his head into the room from the hallway, a brass candlestick in his hand.

"I'm putting this with my other selections, Mrs. J," the man called before ducking back out of view.

"Okay, Gene, I'll write it all up later," she called over her shoulder then looked at Maggie and nodded. "All right, but I don't think this will do either of us any good.

"I came to stay with Albert because he was convinced his dead baby was haunting him. There…not much of a story, is it?"

Maggie felt a chill settle down over her belly. "Why did he think that?"

"Because he was nuts," the old woman chuckled. "That and probably feeling guilty about not being here when Jenny went into lab…took to her bed. Albert had gone down for supplies and the poor little thing was up here all alone. Personally, I don't think he could have done anything to save them if he had been here.

"The doctor said her heart just gave out…sometimes that happens, you know. It wasn't Albert's fault, naturally, but no one could convince him of that."

…sometimes these things happen…

…not his fault…

not HER fault

"But—" Maggie took a deep breath and felt the chill slip farther into her skin. "I still don't understand. Why would Albert think the baby was haunting him?"

The old woman's eyes darted to the hallway as she shook her head.

"Because Albert said the baby was still alive when he found them. It was sticking half way out of Jenny…blue and almost gone…but he said it opened its eyes. Albert was reaching for it when it open its eyes and stared straight at him…and he knew. He said he knew that baby would haunt him for the rest of his life because he hadn't been able to save it. Hadn't given it a chance to be born.

"God, I really must be out of my mind. Please, forgive me…it's just a story. Oh God, I'm so, so sorry!"

Maggie pushed herself to her feet slowly, taking extra care not to bend at the waist. Her hands cradling her belly.

This time she knew she was crying.

"Will you please call my husband," she whispered, the corners of her mouth tipping up into the stream of tears, "I need to go home now."

***

"Little boy blue, come blow your horn, the sheep's in the meadow, the cow's in the corn. But where is the boy who looks after the sheep? He's under the haystack, fast asleep."

Maggie felt the tiny fluttering sensation beneath her ribs and giggled. Old Wigglebutt. Very gently, she pressed her palm just below her navel nub and felt an equally gentle pressure pushing up against it.

"Hon?"

Maggie smiled, watching the darkness behind her eyes turn gold as Sean opened the door.

"What are doing in here? I thought you were going to lie down."

"It's funny," Maggie said, opening her eyes to the soft autumn night beyond the window. The cradle glowed in the light that spilled in from the hallway. "I was tired when I got home but I seem to be just fine now."

She looked back over her shoulder at the dark shape hovering in the doorway. And smiled.

"Pretty amazing, don't you think."

Sean stayed in the doorway like a big, black shadow. Maggie hoped he wouldn't do that once the baby was born. It made him look like some horrible, faceless monster.

"You can't keep doing this to yourself," the faceless monster said, "it's tearing you apart. Besides, you need to rest for tomorrow."

The baby kicked her. Hard enough to make her jump.

"What's the matter?" The monster's voice sounded concerned as it lurched across the room. "Are you all right? Oh, Jesus, the doctor said this kind of thing happens sometimes...what'd he call it...spontaneous abortion, yeah, that's it. God, maybe it's for the best. Come on, hon, stand up and I'll get you to the hospital. Everything'll be okay."

Everything was okay.

Maggie brushed the monster's fingers away when it tried to lifted her up and watched the red-green-white lights of a jet cut across the nighttime sky; imagined the baby laying in his crib watching other jets zoom overhead. There was so much he was going to see.

"Come on, Maggie," the monster snarled, "we have to get to the hospital…you could die just like—"

"Did you hear what you just did? You called me Maggie." Tipping forward, she caressed a lump that had to be a foot…or elbow…it'd been so long she forgot which each felt like. "That's your daddy, by the way. I know he hasn't said much to either of us for a while, but all that's going to change now."

"Oh God, Maggie, what are you doing?" The monster's voice faded as Sean began sobbing. "W-what are you d-doing?"

"Talking to the baby. You're supposed to do that, remember? We read where babies are able to hear a great deal while in utero."

"Maggie, p-please…for Christ's sake, stop it!"

She looked at him, Sean's features shifting back and forth between light and shadow…between the monster and the man she married. The father of her baby.

Of their baby.

"Give me your hand, Sean," she said, holding out her own, then grabbing his when he didn't move fast enough. "It's okay, just here…wait, he moved. There…just press your hand right there."

He almost got away from her, but Maggie held on—forced his clenched fist down against her belly…held her breath while he cursed and screamed and almost became the monster again.

"God DAMMIT, Maggie, what are you trying to

pull? Jesus, you know there's nothing there anymore! W-why are you doing this to us? What are you trying to—"

The baby kicked.

And Maggie felt the trembling fingers unclench.

Slowly.

"Oh, God…Maggie? Maggie, what's going…this can't be happening! It CAN'T."

His fingers spread as wide as they could. The way they used to.

"Maggie, but the baby's…the baby was dead. The doctor showed us. I…I don't understand. We saw the ultrasound. We saw it!"

Maggie saw only the tears streaming down Sean's cheeks.

"Sometimes these things happen," she whispered and laid her hand over his.

Felt the baby stretch from both the inside and out.

She could almost see him yawning, one tiny balled fist rubbing the sleep out of his eyes.

Her little boy blue—her's and Albert's—finally waking up.

HEART OF STONE

Summer had come early to the city and he wanted to be out in it—maybe stroll down to the college and check out a few of the Coffee/Bookstores, or take a self guided tour of the municipal sculpture garden, or listen to some entrepreneurial street band jam, or go to the zoo, or check out if any new acquisitions were to be found in the Antique Shoppes along the upper West Side, or just kick back under a bright leafed cottonwood and watch the girls with winter pale legs walk by, or...or...or.

Or a hundred of the other things he could be doing right now on a beautiful early summer Saturday instead of staring out his Goddamned living room window and waiting for her to finish clearing out her stuff.

He should have known this was going to happen, or at least have expected it from the very beginning. He always seemed to be attracted (in the beginning) to the same kind of woman: Strong and sure and independent on the surface; conniving, clinging "wannabe-wives" from the epidermis down.

Christ.

Refocusing his eyes from the world beyond the glass to the one trapped inside with him, he glared at his own reflection and shook his head.

"When are you ever going to learn?"

A white shape suddenly filled the miniaturized

reflection of the hallway door behind him. She was dressed in white shorts and a matching halter top. As if she were going to play a set of tennis after moving out.

If she ever moved out.

"Did...you say something, Spence?"

Spencer Tolbert shook his head and watched her reflection crumble into tears. Hell, it seemed that's all she'd been doing for the last three days—crying, weeping...begging. And he'd been so nice about it, too; waiting until she'd polished off a very expensive dinner at her favorite restaurant before telling her it was over between them.

But what had that simple act of kindness gotten him? A sudden hysteric who ran sobbing to the Ladies' Room and symbolically threw the meal right back in his face. Followed by a glass-fogging "Question and Answer" session—punctuated liberally with pregnant pauses and phlegmy sobs—through the late night rush hour. Culminating in a final round of echoing hysterics from behind the locked master bathroom door.

It promised to be a long, sleepless night. Fortunately (or not), he'd been through it so many times before—so many, many times before—that he had the procedure down cold.

Thank God.

He had dropped a 'lude, secretively, with their first glass of wine, so that by the time they made it back to his (HIS) apartment, the giddy, pit-of-the-belly tickle was easing into his arms and legs and taking the kinks out of his neck.

While she had sought the sanctuary of the john, Spence barely made it to the couch before his eyes went to half mast and stayed there.

Sometime during the night, he thought he'd heard one of the neighbors pounding on the wall, shouting for someone to shut the hell up.

But he might have been mistaken. Drugs'll do that to you.

Stepping back from the window, Spence glanced down at his watch and frowned. It was just after two in the afternoon. Dammit, the entire day was going to be ruined at this rate.

Even with the drug cocktail, he'd managed to wake up before ten to find her silent, although her face was still bloated from crying, and packing.

Spence took this to be a good sign. He hadn't let her move in all that much stuff…for obvious reasons which were now coming true…so calculated an hour, two at the most, for her to fill up the cardboard boxes she must have gotten while he was still out and vacate his life.

So much for wishful thinking.

"How much longer," he yelled as he caught sight of her in the hallway door again, her bare arms were filled with the pink-and-white towels she had bought their second week together and which he made sure remained safely hidden on the top shelf of the linen closet.

Christ, she was just getting to the linen closet now?

She came back to the doorway and stopped, hugging the towels the way a child would find solace in hugging a teddy bear. The visual analogy turned his stomach.

"I'm sorry this is taking so long," she said stiffly. "If I'd known this was going to happen I could have planned it better."

Jesus. "It's not that," he said, still trying to be nice despite the time she'd already wasted. The thought made him look down at his watch again. "I just wanted to…"

She took the hint. To a point.

"Look, if you have someplace else to go, go. No one's stopping you. I'll be—I'll lock up when I'm finished."

"No, it's okay," Spence sighed, walking slowly

toward the overstuffed chair and ottoman next to the bricked-in fireplace like a man walking the last mile. "I'll wait."

"Really, it's okay you don't have t—" Her face went from concern to suspicion with no stops in between. "You don't trust me, is that it? You think I might slip one of those…things in with my stuff?"

He hadn't thought about it, but ...

Draping himself into the chair, Spence reached over and patted the dog-sized granite gargoyle on the hearth. It was one of the hundreds that filled the apartment and his heart. One of those things she had just mentioned so eloquently.

He'd been collecting the grotesque figurines for years, long before they became "fashionable". Although he had to admit that now that they had, his collection was probably worth hundreds of thousands of dollars.

If he ever decided to sell it.

Which he never would.

At least not until he grew tired of his life as a perpetual Art History student closing in on forty or the school kicked him out for dating most of the female faculty members under sixty or his vast collection of scholarships petered out and he had to find a real job.

Then he'd see.

But until that day arrived (if it ever did) they were his to love and cherish and keep as cobweb free as humanly possible: From the smallest, a Mount St. Helens pressed ash novelty he'd found in an airport gift shop, to the giant, man-sized stone behemoth he had saved from a demolition crew's wrecking ball and which now hung suspended in a cat's-cradle of reinforced wires from the ceiling over his bed.

It was particularly impressive with the recessed spot light shining directly behind it.

Spence had watched many a co-dependent hopeful look up at the twisted limbs and leering snake-like face dangling just a few feet overhead and seen the passion drain from their face.

Of course, as evidenced by his current situation and the many (many) others that preceded it, the system was not totally fool-proof.

"Is that why you're sticking around, Spence?" she asked again. "To make sure I don't steal anything?"

"Of course not...um—" He'd forgotten her name. "It's just that—" That what, whatsyourface? "—it looks better if I stay."

Lame. Very, very lame. And Spence could tell by the look on her face that she—L. Her name started with an L. Lilly? Louise? Lulu?—knew it, too.

Christ, how could he have forgotten her name already? Usually it took a week to ten days after the woman left before he forgot her name. Well, Spence said mentally to the lion-faced gargoyle staring loyally up at him, just proves I probably waited a week too long.

There was understanding in the stone face. That, and just the faintest hint of worldliness in the gaping smile. It understood, all right. A man's gotta do what a man's gonna do.

Spence traced the smile with the tips of his fingers.

"Do you mind looking at me when I'm talking to you?"

She was still framed in the doorway when Spence looked up. He patted the gargoyle's head again and the soft hand-against-stone sound filled the momentary silence. Outside, summer beckoned.

"Sorry," he lied, "I thought you'd stopped talking."

Her eyes filled at that, reflecting the sunlight pouring in through the window. God, how he wanted to be out in it.

"You're not going to make this any easier, are you, Spence?"

He shrugged. Damn, why was she still here? Couldn't she understand that he'd already distanced himself from her...from...

Leah! Her name was Leah—something ethnic.

"Look, Leah," he said the name as if he'd known it all along, "this is hard on both of us, okay? I'm just as broken up about this as you are. I mean I really thought this thing was go...going t..."

It probably would have been a lot better if his body hadn't chosen that exact moment to yawn.

Her tears dried instantly.

"You bastard," she—Leah—hissed before disappearing back into the bedroom. An instant later there came the sounds of minor demolition: Bangs and thumps and wire coat-hangers being rattled like the swords of an advancing army.

But, at least it sounded like she was finally packing. At long last.

Spence shook his head at the stone monstrosity before using it to lever himself from the chair. Another thump, followed by the sound of something heavy hitting the floor and a loud curse, echoed down the short hallway.

Maybe it would be better if he left. Just for a little while. Give her a chance to leave with some part of her dignity (and his facial features) intact.

"Okay, look," Spence said as he walked to the front door, pausing only long enough to scoop his keys from the curled tongue of the Green Man on the coffee table. "I can see you'd really rather be alone right now, so..."

He had his hand on the brass door-knob, a smirking satyr he'd found in a renovation catalogue, when Leah appeared in the doorway. She was holding a gift-wrapped package about a foot square. Both the paper and large satin ribbon were in variegated shades of gold.

The fact that the package might actually only be a cleverly disguised front for a cocked and loaded revolver which she was even now aiming at his belly, was only a passing thought when he saw that both her hands were needed to hold the box. Whatever was in there was heavy.

"I was going to give you this for...I don't know, maybe our six months anniversary." She shrugged and smiled, tried to smile. Spence gave her partial credit for the effort and smiled back.

"But I guess we're not going to have one. So here..." She held out the box as she came toward him, then moved back to the door when he accepted it.

It was heavy.

Spence shook it, gently, kid-sneaking-a-shake-on-Christmas-Eve gently and felt something shift inside.

"I really shouldn't. You know, all things considered..."

He kept his smile in place and offered her the package, watching her reaction. She just leaned against the door frame and shrugged again. There was no screaming or covering vital body parts or sudden dashes for cover.

It was just a gift after all.

"No, really," she said, "I want you to have it. I know how much you like these things and ..." Shrug. The beginning of tears. "As a remembrance of our time together, okay?"

Spence fought the urge to roll his eyes as he set the box on one arm of the couch, the only semi-uncluttered spot he could find, and began ripping it apart. The joy of anticipation had never been high on his list of pleasures.

The gold paper gave way to a pristine white box that yielded blood red tissue. The whole color scheme made

Spence feel as if he were disemboweling some kind of animal.

An animal of paper with a white marble heart.

"God," he said softly as he lifted the heart out with his hands, "it's beautiful...I mean it's butt ugly, but, you know. Where did you get it?"

Spence was only interested so he could make a mental note to go back and visit the store again. If it had any more treasures like this...

"A little place over on either Magnolia or Elm, I'm not sure. I saw it in the window and thought you'd like it."

Spence nodded without looking up. "I love it," he said, and for the first time in their relationship, past and present, meant it.

It was a gargoyle—naturally; she wasn't anything if not observant, and, after all, she had been with him almost three months—but a gargoyle the likes of which Spence had never seen before.

The size of two fists clenched tightly together, it was a hodge-podge of the classic "grotesque" style: The head of a cherub, serene; eyes closed, lips parted in a wide, toothless frown, sat hunched upon the body of a pig; the carved "flesh" puddling in loose folds around the baboon-like naked rump and piggy back hooves. Bat-like wings were curled in tight against knobby shoulders that looked like miniature mountain ranges, and two rudimentary hands, consisting of only a thumb and articulated claw held twin pieces of a shattered human heart against its chest. Even the marble was unlike any he'd ever seen before; it was cut through with veins of a pink/gray/black ore that sparkled when it caught the light and had a buttery smooth texture more like jade than marble.

All in all it was the ugliest, most distorted, perverted mockery of nature Spence had ever seen.

He loved it.

"Wow," he said before he could catch himself. Cradling the heavy little monstrosity against his belly, Spence regained control of his enthusiasm and looked up. "Thanks, Leah. I really like it."

Which, he could tell by her reaction, wasn't exactly what she'd hoped to hear from him.

"Yeah. Well, okay then," she said. "Guess I'd better finish." But didn't move a muscle to leave. "Yeah."

Spence watched her, not moving, for another full minute before showing how it was done and carrying his newest treasure to a place of honor on the wide ledge in front of the window. Backlit by the warm summer sunlight the frowning, sightless face looked all the more angelic...the body all the more grotesque.

She was still leaning against the door frame when he turned around.

"I think I will go out," he told her, not stopping until he'd opened the apartment door and had one foot out into the hall. "You can leave your key on my desk or drop it off at the Super's. Either way's fine."

"Okay." And she actually moved. Pushed away from the wall and...Stopped. "Oh. Do you mind if I leave a couple things here? I mean, I promise I'll have them picked up tomorrow...when you're at work. I'll get the Super to let me in and he can watch me to make sure I don't..." Her voice broke.

"D-do you think that would be okay?"

Spence didn't remember her bringing anything that would require an entire separate trip in order to move, but nodded anyway. Hell, it was probably easier than whatever the alternative would turn out to be.

"Sure. No problem. Make sure the door's locked when you leave. See ya."

Something thumped against the inside of the door as he left, but since the sound wasn't immediately followed by anything more important than a wailing sob, Spence ignored it.

***

He'd stayed out longer than he'd wanted to.

Twilight was almost putting out the sunset's fire when he fit his key into the lock only to discover that she, Leah Something-ethnic, hadn't bothered to lock the dead-bolt. Figured. She might be gone but she was damned sure she wasn't going to be forgotten.

His late arrival back to the apartment had also been because of her. A little shop on either Magnolia or Elm— Hah! The only buildings on both Magnolia and Elm were abandoned and boarded up or in the process of being abandoned and boarded up. Wherever it was that she got the gargoyle it definitely wasn't in a little shop on either Magnolia or Elm.

Spence thought about leaving a note for her with the Super as to where the elusive shop was, then decided against it. A note would lead to a phone call which would lead to another phone call and on and on and on. Yadda, yadda.

Nope, he thought closing and locking the door behind him, that was too high a price to pay even for the hopes of discovering another find like the angle-faced gargoyle.

Spence tossed his keys back into the waiting Green Man's gaping mouth and walked quickly to the window. The angle-faced gargoyle looked up at him, serenity spilling from the large empty pupils.

Picking it up, Spence ran a thumb over both eyes.

The marble felt cool in his hands despite having basked in the sun all afternoon, the carved eyes almost cold against his skin.

Were the eyes always open?

He couldn't remember. He'd thought they were closed, but, hell, he'd been in such a hurry to vacate the apartment he was lucky he remembered as much as he did.

Chucking it under its sullen little mouth, Spence set it back on the window sill. The outstretched wings clinked softly against the glass when he noticed his extra set of keys sitting on the edge of his writing desk.

Well, at least that was one other thing he wouldn't have to worry about.

Whistling happily to himself, he swiped the keys into the top desk drawer and took himself into the kitchen for a celebratory glass of wine.

He'd forgotten her name again by the second glass.

***

The soft, rhythmic thumping of lovemaking woke him up.

"Jesus Christ," he moaned, rolling over to bury his head beneath the pillow after catching sight of the glowing numbers on the digital clock/radio next to the bed. "It's four-fucking-thirty in the morning…what are you people? Vampires? Screw in the daylight, for God's sake."

Another series of thumps answered him, but the pillow's muffling effect made it bearable.

Somewhat.

Spence had almost fallen back to sleep when the crash jerked him into full consciousness. That definitely wasn't the sound of lovemaking, unless a pair of Apache Dancers had moved in next door without him knowing about it.

And it was too close. Living room close.

His living room.

Sweat was beginning to ooze down over his forehead when Spence heard a softer thump followed by an unmistakably feminine sigh.

The bitch! Ethnic-Whatsherface. It had to be. He hadn't really looked at the set of keys she left. Hell only knew if they belonged to the apartment or not.

"Shit!" He whispered the word just loud enough to make sure he was fully awake, but not so loud as to be heard in the next room. If she'd planned a surprise visit, then by God she was going to get a surprise visit!

Feet kicking at the sleep tangled sheets, Spence reached down and pulled the Louisville Slugger from its place beside the headboard. It was a gift from yet another admirer, an early one who'd lived in the big city all her life but was still afraid of guns. The bat had been a compromise. Spence had originally wanted a machete with a gargoyle face carved into the handle.

He bought the machete a week later, after the "bat-lady" moved out.

A slow shuffling came from the far right corner of the room when Spence opened the bedroom door. Bat locked firm against his shoulder, fingers tightening into a choke, bare ass molding itself to the molding, he held his breath and squinted into the darkness.

The light from the street was just bright enough to draw the demarcation lines between the front window and the walls. The rest of the room was layered, shadow upon shadow.

Maybe it really had been the neighbors pretending to be love starved minks.

Spence exhaled loudly.

And a sigh answered him.

Shit! "All right…" What was her name? "…you. I don't know what you think this'll accomplish, but even with that set of keys you lied about giving back, this whole thing amounts to breaking and entering." Nothing. "Look, I took three years of Criminal Law before Art History, so I know what I'm talking about." Not a sound. "Hey. Are you listening?"

Yep, she was. A paperback, by the fluttering sound it made, thumped to the floor next to the bookcase in the far corner.

God, he really could pick'em.

"All right, don't say I didn't warn you."

Tightening his grip on the bat with his right hand, Spence reached out with his left and began patting the wall on that side for the overhead light-switch. He could still hear her, moving slowly, tentatively in the darkness, but wasn't able to catch even the faintest hint of movement. She'd either done this before, sneaking into ex-lover's apartments at night, or was a natural born cat burglar.

Another book thumped to the floor. Followed by one of the gargoyle bookends he kept on the second shelf. Followed by the downstairs neighbor, a crotchety old fart literature professor, thumping on the floor/ceiling with a broom handle.

Well, maybe not a natural born burglar.

When his thumb found the raised plastic cover-plate, Spence squeezed his eyelids shut and pulled his chin in toward his chest. He wanted the sudden intrusion of light to blind only one of the people in the room. And he was going to make sure that one wasn't going to be him.

Five, four, three-two-one BLAST OFF! And flipped the switch.

The space on the other side of his eyelids remained dark.

What the—?

Spence flipped the toggle three more times, getting the same results—nothing—before easing his eyes open. The room was exactly as he'd left it. Dark. Shit, what a time for the bulb to burn out.

Re-shouldering the bat, Spence leaned forward and slowly walked toward the ceramic gargoyle lamp on the end table next to the couch. On the fifth step the sole of his left foot encountered the reason why the overhead light hadn't gone on. The bulb hadn't burned out, the fixture had been shattered into a hundred pieces and he'd just found the largest one.

His startled yelp brought another series of ceiling/floor thumps; but that worried him less than the blood he could already feel seeping around the glass shard in his foot.

"Goddammit!"—thump, thump—Shuffle. "Look, I wasn't mad until now," Yeah, right. "But you've gone too far now. I had to put down a security deposit on this place and you're going to pay for the light. Do you hear me?"

Shuffle—thump, THUMP—

Hopping, using the bat as a makeshift cane, Spence made it to the couch without any more glass fragments finding their way into his flesh. This time, however, he hadn't taken the precaution of shutting his eyes before turning on the lamp, and the momentary white-out stung almost as badly as the wound in his foot.

"SHIT!"

—THUMP THUMP—

"Shut up," Spence yelled to the floor as he pried his eyelids open just enough to be able to see the blurry, bloody projectile sticking out of the bottom of his foot. It wasn't a big shard, but it was slippery from the blood and hurt like hell when he was finally able to yank it out. "Shut up. Shut up. Shut-the-fuck-up!"

There wasn't a sound from the floor/ceiling. In fact, the only sound in the apartment was the soft, slow drip of his blood against the hardwood floor and the equally soft and slow shuffling from the shadows across the room.

Spence sat on the arm of the couch, alternately rubbing his eyes and his foot, the bat well within reach, when he noticed another sound; the rhythmic bump-thump that had originally woken him up. His neighbors were at it again, blessedly humping away unaware of the drama taking place only a lathe-and-plaster width away.

He would have shouted at them to shut-the-fuck-up as well…if it hadn't suddenly come crawling out of the shadows.

Spence's hand dropped, unnoticed, to his lap. It was impossible. Impossible.

But there it was. Alive. Impossible. Dragging itself steadily toward him. Impossible. The little piggy hooves were all but useless, tangled beneath the quivering folds of naked white flesh, too small to support a body that seemed larger in flesh than it had in stone; it moved by dragging itself along with its wings, extending one, then the other until it reached the edge of the pool of light in front of the couch.

It stopped there, wings curling in tight against its misshapen body, and looked up at Spence, blinking; holding out the two pieces of the broken heart it clutched in its…"hands."

A small stream of black blood spurted from the halves with each straining beat. It wasn't the sound of his neighbors making love that woke Spence up…

"Oh, God," he whispered.

It hissed back—the lower jaw unhinging, the sound broken into a thousand fragments by the sharply pointed teeth Spence hadn't noticed before.

It hissed again when Spence grabbed for the bat, its wings snapping open like a shotgun blast as it leapt into the air.

It was surprisingly agile...surprisingly fast for something shaped like a canned ham with wings—slicing through the air in one direction only to drop one wing, tumble, stoop and come straight at Spence from another angle.

And each time it came at him he swung at it, certain—until the bat whistled through empty air—that he'd connect.

"God damn you!" he screamed at it, "stay still!"

Thumps, bangs and closed-fist poundings were coming in from all sides now, except the ceiling...his ceiling...but then the gargoyle was taking care of that area. On the second pass at Spence's head, it had to do a sharp right turn to avoid the bat and took out the rest of the broken ceiling light.

On the fourth and fifth passes, it knocked over the Green Man and destroyed the tiny dragon-faced gargoyle wall sconce over the TV.

"You fucking bastard!"

It paused in mid-air, wings laboring to keep it aloft, and laughed at him.

Spence knocked over the table lamp, shattering the bulb and plunging the room back into shadows, as he took a step forward and swung. The pain in his foot reached his brain only a split second before a newer, sharper pain overrode it.

The thing had come in low, riding the crest of the sudden darkness, and tore open Spence's chest with its teeth. He could see the twin, pock marked crescent wounds just above his heart as dawn brightened the sky.

"Goddammitsonofabitchwhore!"

He could hear its wheezing laughter as he cocked and swung—

CRACK

It felt as if he'd connected with a steel wrecking ball. Hands, wrists, elbows, shoulders and rib cage trembling from the impact, Spence dropped the stump of the broken bat and stumbled at an oblique angle toward the desk. His first intention was to call the police, daring them not to believe him; but when he finally got there and looked back at the thing on the floor, he wondered if that would be such a good idea.

The growing brightness made the carnage in front of him all that much harder to ignore. And made all that had happened just a moment before (Had it?) even harder to believe. There were pieces of gargoyle strewn halfway to the bedroom door. Although some of it was still recognizable— a broken claw-hand holding a chipped carved heart, the left hind foot-bottom wing-and-wrinkled butt portion, the talon-tipped end of a wing—most of the statue had been reduced to marble dust.

The head had come off as a single chunk. It was lying, upside down, wedged against the bottom of the couch. The angelic face serene. The eyes closed.

"What the hell?" he said softly, his voice rising with each limping step he took. "What the hell? What the Hell? WHAT THE H—"

Spence's neighbors were starting their own shouting match when the sun finally peeked out from behind the rooftops opposite his apartment and pinned him in place like a bug on a killing board.

The next "What the hell" was whispered as he looked down and watched his body, from just below his belly button shift from flesh tone to dove gray and harden to stone.

"I—I can't...this can't—"

Spence twisted at the waist and felt the air hiss uselessly from his lungs. The stone covering his back and legs was different. Large, sharp protrusions erupted from both ankles, curving down and around feet that now resembled lion's paws.

This can't be happening. This can't be happening. His brain kept up the liturgy until Spence made the mistake of looking straight into the sun.

The pounding sounded very far away after that.

***

Fall had come early.

He knew that even if he couldn't see the leaves changing colors or hear the geese flying overhead, or feel the night lengthening just a little more each day. The place where he stood was ringed by black solar panels, he couldn't see past them...couldn't see past the barrier of white light.

But he knew fall had come.

He could see her.

She came every day, Leah Something-ethnic, sometimes to stand and admire, sometimes just to sit on one of the uncomfortable little marble benches the city provided and whisper about things he could no longer see, or, sometimes when she was in a particularly happy mood, to sketch his likeness on a thick drawing pad.

She always showed him the drawings: A twisted monstrosity, hunched over on itself, one clawed hand raised in front of a face that was neither Lion nor Green Man nor Dragon but a warped combination of all three. The perfect gargoyle, snarling in wide mouthed anger at the entire world.

He knew fall had come early because of her. The way her clothing had changed from the bright, flowing sun dress she'd worn the day she presented him to the city's statue garden (insuring constant viewing pleasure by the ring of solar-powered lights she herself paid for), to the drab browns and gray tweeds and turtlenecks she now wore on her daily visits.

Spence could feel her moving just beyond the lights now, could feel her footsteps against the concrete walk as she approached.

It was fall. Soon it would be winter…and with the winter would come the long, dark nights of snow and howling winds.

Ever since Spence could remember, a winter hadn't gone by without at least one city wide power failure.

He could wait.

Her footsteps echoed through the stone in his ears as she stepped through the cage of lights. She was looking up at him. And smiling.

Spence wished he could smile back.

HERE THERE BE DRAGONS

Dr. Leo Matthias studied a rat-grey pigeon waddling the ledge outside his office window, then returned his gaze to the dapper old man sitting across from him.

"Would you mind repeating that, sir."

"No, of course not. I would like a Paranoid-Schizophrenic with Delusions of Grandeur, please," he answered. "To go."

"Ah."

The handy professional "Space Saver" was promptly marred by a quick note. In Leo's $125.00-an hour opinion, the old man had undoubtedly described his own mental aberration.

Which was something, at least.

Leo had walked into his office that morning to find the old man sitting behind his desk, calmly leafing through the latest issue of Psychology Today. The receptionist swore she hadn't let him in and his appointment book showed no one scheduled for another hour. But the polished nails, neatly trimmed beard and $500.00 Brook's Brothers suit...along with the unusual request...peaked Leo's financial if not professional curiosity.

"For any particular reason, Mr...?" Leo put down the antique ebony fountain pen to make eye contact. Usually that was enough to initiate dialogue.

Today it wasn't.

The old man looked straight back. And winked.

"Well, of course there's a reason, doctor. To make such a request without reason would be…madness."

You can say that again, buster. "And what would that reason be?"

"To participate in a quest."

Leo picked up his pen. "For what?"

"The Holy Grail, sir."

"Ah-hah." He wrote Don Quixote on the note pad and underlined it twice. "And may I ask why you've decided to look for a Paranoid-Schizophrenic with Delusions of Grandeur for so lofty a mission? It would seem to me that a Knight Errant would be the more appropriate choice."

Leo never tried to argue or bully a patient out of an illusion—It ended the sessions too quickly and cut into profits.

"Welllll…" The old man chuckled and tugged on one corner of his beard. "Actually, it was Gordon Bradshaw's idea."

"Gordon Brad—" Leo set the pen down carefully and leaned back in his chair, moving his foot toward the recessed "Alarm" button under his desk. One never knew when even the most sedate patient would become violent. "You mean the mass murderer?"

The old man found a piece of lint on the sleeve of his jacket and just as carefully removed it.

"Yes," he said, without looking up. "Not that he was my first choice, mind you; but you would be surprised at the number of good men who refused me."

When he finally looked up, the old man's face was slack with sorrow.

"They lacked the courage, you see…so I finally decided to go against tradition and look for men with—well, with perhaps less than a heroic reputation, but who have

demonstrated the courage to go against society's norm."
Deep set eyes, the color of Leo's pen, sparkled as he spoke.
"Gordon Bradshaw seemed a likely candidate; given that
criteria. He proved even less willing to co-operate than the
others had. However, he did offer me an option I had previ-
ously over-looked."

"And that was?" Leo asked

"Well, to paraphrase the man's colloquial terminol-
ogy…he was of the opinion that a man would have to be
crazy to accept my offer.

"He then went on to suggest I engage in an activity
which was physically impossible—considering how the
neck is attached to the body ..."

"Ah." Leo moved his foot away from the alarm and
picked up his pen. The old man was a loon—plain and simple and harmless. Gordon Bradshaw would no more be
allowed visitors than he would be given a flaying knife and
bag of candy and told to go back to collecting children.

"Oh, and by the way, I don't think myself to be Don
Quixote. He was a literary character spawned from imagina-
tion and fancy. I am quite real."

Leo chuckled and turned the pad over. Well, the old
boy's got excellent eyes, I'll give him that.

"I have excellent eyes, Dr. Matthias. As befits my
name."

Coincidence. "Ah…I mean, yes, Mr ..."

"Myrddin Merlinus Emrys—the Falcon." He
paused for effect. "But you may call me Merlin."

Leo had to fight the urge to clap his hands together.
Yes!

"THE Merlin? Like in *Le Morte d'Arthur*?"

A cloud suddenly blocked the sun and Leo heard
the distant rumble of thunder echo through the deep high-
rise canyons of glass and steel. Out of the corner of his eye,

he saw the fat ledge-walking pigeon take to the air. A single feather, lost in flight, swirled in the gusting air.

"Yes," the old man said softly, "that Merlin."

Leo swallowed carefully, as visions of T-Bills and Time Shares danced in his head.

"But I thought you'd been trapped in the Crystal Cave by whatshername..." Leo snapped his fingers as if he'd just remembered. "Morganna LeFey."

A brilliant white light, followed by a sizzling crack and the smell of ozone, filled the room. When the after image faded, Leo watched five more feathers—scorched and smoldering—spiral downward past the window.

"The bitch."

Leo blinked as a charred lump followed the feathers descent. "What?"

The old man twisted a corner of his moustache while a small tic began Mamboing under his left eye. Leo dutifully added the information to his notes.

"I gave her the gifts of enchantment out of love and she ..." A weary smile eased the tension from his face. "You have a saying that fits the situation I believe—There's no fool like an old fool. Unflattering, but unfortunately so true. I believe she's now selling Real Estate."

Leo set the pad aside, after jotting down the time and adding an hour's "Inconvenience Time", and folded his hands.

"Well, we've made an excellent start, Mr...Merlin. And one that I'm sure we can continue to work through in the—" Years "—sessions to come. But now...if you'll excuse me, I do have other patients to see."

The old man didn't move except to drape one leg over the other. Getting comfortable. Goddammit. Leo stood up to show him how it was done and took a step toward the door.

"Just make an appointment with my receptionist." He smiled. Took another step. Went so far as to nod.

The old man nodded back. And stayed seated.

"Sir…"

"No, I'm afraid I was never knighted. True I am Arthur's cousin and counsel, but I thought it best not to place myself beneath his will. He needed a strong hand and if I were knighted …"

"Enough." Leo was toying with the idea of breaking one of his own rules and toss the potential Swiss Bank Account out on his ear. "The session, sir, is over. If you'd like to come back and talk to me about these delusions of yours—"

"Delusions?"

"—then make an appointment. Or, if you prefer, my receptionist can give you the name of another doctor equally qualified to treat your—condition. Either way, I'm afraid I must ask you to leave. Sir."

Leo had his hand on the door-knob when he turned around. The old man was standing: Red faced, closed fists, set jaw…but standing…

The old man drew himself up and squared his shoulders. Leo had originally placed him at about 5'7"-5'8"…now he seemed closer to six feet. And heavier. Much heavier. Flesh seemed to be filling the wrinkles from the inside out.

"I am not psychotic, good doctor…nor will I leave until I have obtained that for which I have come."

The man's voice was deeper than it had been a moment before, and carried a lilting British accent. Leo mentally applauded the transformation—it took a real sickie to produce details like that—and opened the door a crack. If there were any threats going to be made, he wanted his receptionist to be able to testify later on.

"That's right, you wanted a paranoid-schizophrenic with delusions of grandeur." He patted the breast and side pockets of his sports coat with his free hand. "Sorry, fresh out. But just for your edification, sir, I'm not in the habit of handing out my patients. Even to the Wizard of King Arthur's court.

"Now get the hell out of my office before I have you physically ejected!"

Leo threw open the door and came face to slavering jaws with a dragon. Or, at least it appeared to be a dragon for the few nano-seconds he stared up into it's bile-green eyes.

All three of them.

The door felt less than adequate as he slammed it shut and leaned back against it...considering the amount of snarling and clawing coming from the other side.

"What the Hell is that?"

"A pet."

As if encouraged by the sound of it's master's voice, the "pet" tried to drive the doorknob through Leo's spine. He barely felt it. Something far more interesting was happening in front of him.

The dark blue business suit which had fit the old man so perfectly a moment before suddenly looked ten sizes too big. It hung from his body—bunching at his ankles and elbows like a poorly chosen Goodwill hand-me-down.

In the brief respite between snarls and guttural hisses from the reception area, Leo heard a gentle ripping sound and watched the seams simultaneously tear themselves apart. The strips of material fluttered against the old man as if buffeted by a gentle breeze, then slowly melted into one another.

A mewling sound curled through the door just behind Leo's right ear as the old man took a step forward.

The hem of the midnight blue gown whispered

against the nap of the carpet as he stopped. Crude symbols stitched across the bodice and shoulders glimmered beneath the high-intensity track lights. The old man cocked his head and let his hand caress the sheathed knife—grip bound in leather, a milky-white stone set in the pommel—hanging at his waist. The tip of the sleeve, wide and full and edged in crimson, brushed against the arm of a chair and left a chard, blackened swath in it's wake.

A thin coil of silver, crafted to resemble a living snake, curled around the old man's forehead. Leo caught a flash of emerald green from the thing's eyes as the old man turned and slowly walked to the window. He shook his head as he looked out, arms crossed over his chest…wisps of smoke curling upward from the hems of his sleeves.

"There are no more heros, doctor" he said without turning around. "It is a sad fact but one I cannot allow myself to dwell upon. Come here."

Leo wasn't about to move away from the door but discovered he had little choice in the matter. He glided over the plush 100-percent virgin wool without moving a muscle.

"Look down there."

Leo's nose squashed into the double pane glass.

"Seven point three million people…and not one of them with the balls God gave a gnat."

Leo gurgled.

"No. No, don't try to justify their poor showing to me," the old man flicked a finger and Leo slid off the glass like a slug, "You people have been industrialized, sanitized, civilized…lobotomized into accepting one and only one reality."

He uncrossed his arms with a flourish. Smoldering etches appeared in the glass where his sleeves brushed against it.

"I offered them another realm."

Leo worked his jaw with one hand until he was satisfied it wasn't broken.

"There's a name for that," he said, "it's called Fantasy. We have special places for people who live there."

The old man turned his head and smiled. "And dost thou not believe what thy eyes tell thee?"

"What? That you really are Merlin? Give me a break, okay." Standing, Leo brushed past the old man and seated himself behind his desk. While giving the outward appearance of a calm professional from the waist up, his left foot was tap-dancing with gusto on the concealed alarm. Ten minutes...fifteen on the outside, if the building security guard was in the john...and the old man would be history.

But, in the meantime...

"I'll admit the suit trick wasn't bad." Leo offered a half-dozen perfunctory claps. "Bra—vo. Although I have to admit I saw it done better at a local Comedy Club. Guy turned into a gorilla. Great effect...now that was magic!"

A fist-sized ball of lightning crashed into the window directly next to Leo's skull. Silver spider-webs appeared in the glass.

"Dost thou think this magic?" The old man leaped onto the desk seemingly without effort and glared down at Leo. The headband's tiny green eyes flashed. "Magic is an illusion, doctor, a parlour trick any dolt could perform. I am a Sorcerer."

"And one hell of an actor," he mumbled, double timing the alarm button. There'd be no question about the man's sanity when the guard rushed in—thank God. One look and the old coot would be hog-tied and headed for the nearest Mental Reclamation Center.

Clearing his throat, Leo removed his pen from under the old man's left foot and tapped it against his chin. "My apologies. I'm just not used to having Fifth Century

Sorcerers popping in for a chat."

"Sixth Century, to be exact."

The old man jumped backward off the desk with the agile grace of a cat and sat down...hovered actually, in mid-air three feet off the ground. Leo smiled, having seen Mimes pretend to sit on invisible chairs many times before.

The explanation faltered however when the old man raised his feet onto an invisible ottoman. Leo hadn't even seen David Copperfield try that one.

"Now, back to business," he said, getting comfortable, "simply give me what I have come for, doctor and I'll be on my way."

"Well, I...it...I mean..." Taking a deep breath, Leo picked up his pen and slowly—thoughtfully—began tapping it against his chin as his feet went into overdrive under the desk. "I cannot simply give you one of my patient's ..."

Thunder deepened the cracks in the window. A crystal shard fell to the carpet.

"...I mean without a good reason."

The old man—Merlin—considered it for a moment and nodded.

"All right, then I shall explain. Again. I require someone who will not become overly upset if...reality should suddenly change. Become fantastic. And what better choice then someone who doesn't have a clear grasp on either?"

Leo frowned. That kind of thinking could be bad for business. "But that's crazy."

Merlin smiled and a golden beam of sunlight poured into the room. The office door vibrated with a low throaty purr.

"Exactly, doctor. I've tried this before with men renowned for their wisdom and knowledge...and look what it got me. Death, dismemberment, betrayal, royal bloodlines severed for all time...Myself set down for all history as a doddering old fool done in by a pair of shapely thighs—

"But not this time. This time I shall choose the Defenders of the Faith." He glanced toward the window as another splinter of glass fell. "Not leave it up to a still-green boy with more of his brains below his belt than under his crown."

Leo snuck a quick peek at his Rolex. Any time now...any time...

"Am I keeping you from another appointment, doctor?" The old man asked courteously.

"NO...no, not at all." Leo swallowed and straightened his tie—almost poking out his eye with the pen in the process. "Now...about this quest —"

"For the Grail."

"Yes. Isn't it...well, a bit ambitious?"

Merlin crossed his arms over his chest and huffed loudly. The purr behind the door instantly turned vicious. Leo glared. Whoever it was in the dragon costume was going to get theirs soon enough. He just wanted the privilege of signing the commitment papers.

"Now you sound just like Arthur."

Leo's gaze drifted back to the seemingly floating psychotic.

"Arthur?"

"The King."

"Ah."

"No, Arthur didn't think too much of the quest first time around. He even had the nerve to try and convince me that the Grail was nothing more than a myth. Convince me ...ME who taught him how to wipe his nose. HAH!"

Three more pieces of window tumbled to the floor as the old man's accomplice echoed the thunder from out in the reception area. Where the hell WAS that guard?

"But not this time," Merlin said slowly as if measuring his words. "This time we shall find the Holiest of Chalices and set history straight."

"Well, I wouldn't worry too much about that if I were you…Merlin." The name left a bad taste in his mouth. "Every kid knows the story about King Arthur and the Quest. Hell…there've been books written about it, movies made…even a really great musical—"

An entire panel of glass struck the floor and shattered. "Yes…and my character didn't even get one bloody song. No. The Grail is still missing and it was my sworn quest to retrieve it."

Levitating until the top of his head brushed the acoustic ceiling, Merlin uncurled one long nailed finger and pointed it directly at Leo's still throbbing nose.

"Wilt thou give me that which I seek?"

Jaw unhinged, and sphincter threatening to follow suit, Leo quickly went through his mental list of paranoid-schizophrenics with or without delusions of grandeur, and came up empty handed. Nothing.

Not one paranoid or schizophrenic or delusionist. The majority of his practice seemed to consist entirely of burned-out Baby-Boomers who were troubled by the fact that their fathers never cried.

Shit.

"Ummmm."

"Doctor," the floating apparition growled, "bring forth that which I have asked or suffer the consequences."

"Ahhh…"

"Doc? Hey, doc?" A powerfully masculine voice called. "Are you okaaaa—?"

The question lengthened into a bubbling scream which ended in a wet smack.

Leo shoved the chair backwards and stood up. "What the hell was that?"

Black eyes focused on Leo's face. "My pet was getting peckish so I allowed you to order his lunch."

The guard. Purrs mixed with slurping crunches vibrated through the door.

"Well, doctor?"

"Well this, asshole."

Leo made it to the small office bathroom just as the outer door exploded inward. Better to be found hiding like a naughty little boy than to face whatever had just burst into the room. The rational portion of Leo's mind concluded it was probably Gordon Bradshaw inside the elaborate costume; the other ninety nine percent refused to comment.

Leo glanced back just as the thing regurgitated a ball of liquid fire. He could feel the heat liquefying his flesh as he fell backwards...

...onto a clover strewn knoll.

The sunlight overhead stung his eyes, making them water. Lifting one arm to shield his face he scraped his cheek raw with the studded leather glove.

"Careful, boy, I've no use for a one-eyed knight."

Leo blinked around the glare and pain. Merlin was standing a few yards away, leaning on a gnarled staff. A small hawk...no, a falcon glared down at Leo from the old man's shoulder.

"What the fuck?"

"Very good, doctor...speaking like a native Saxon all ready. Excellent. You'll make a fine Sixth Century Knight."

Leo stood up...tried to stand up. He was wearing a stiff leather tunic over-laid with sheets of hammered metal linked together with rings. Beneath it, next to his naked skin, was a coarsely spun jumper made of raw wool. His legs were bare, his feet wrapped in shapeless leather boots.

"Knight?"

"Of course." A deep chuckle caused the little bird to ruffle it's feathers. "Why, you really didn't believe in those 'knights in shining armor' fairy stories, did you?"

Merlin crossed the distance between them in three strides and squatted, using his staff as a balance.

"Sorry to disappoint you, doctor. But this is reality: Pair-of-plate armor, studded leather, hand to hand combat with short swords. Mud, blood and outdoor facilities…" The smile widened on his face. "And the quest for the Holy Grail."

Leo tried to scoot backwards only to run into a half buried rock. It hurt too bad to be an illusion. "What do you want with me?"

Merlin stood up and took a deep breath. "Again, not my first choice, but beggars cannot be choosers. Besides, my friend, you do have some of what I've been seeking. After building your own fantasy world of expensive cars, gold wrist-watches and investment properties, assimilating mine will be relatively easy. You see doctor, you do qualify in a way. See your destiny, sir! These are not mere trappings and delusions, I'm offering you a chance at achieving true grandeur!"

Lifting the staff, he raised it over Leo's head. The sun seemed to surround him. "Thou hast been chosen, Sir Knight, for thy valor and courage to seek the Holiest of Grails. How speaks thee?"

"You're nuts." Leo pulled his legs in under him, tried to push himself and fell back under Merlin's staff. "Okay, so you're not nuts…you're just a real good hypnotist or illusionist or you slipped something into my morning coffee when I wasn't looking or you planned this with my wife to get my insurance money or—" Leo licked his lips, tasted dirt and grimaced. "Or I'm crazy."

Merlin shook his head and moved the staff away.

"No, you're not crazy, doctor, I assure you. I am Merlin, this is the sixth century, and you will seek the Holy Grail. And this time, with luck and by the grace of God, we shall succeed in our quest."

"And if we don't?" Leo asked.

The smile twitched again as the falcon took flight.

"Then I shall have to keep trying." Bending down, the old man offered Leo his hand and pulled him to his feet. "There now, shall we be away Sir Lyonel? Methinks, I remember a banquet being planned in thy honor. Percival brought down a stag this morn for the sole purpose, and Arthur himself has ordered new mead served up."

Leo looked into the old man's eyes—deep hollows that led into the man's soul.

"But stay close, Sir Lyonel, and do not tarry in the deepening shadows." Merlin smiled and tossed an arm lightly over Leo's shoulders. "Here there be dragons."

LETTING GO

Jenna came back with the first snow of the season.

Cody had just opened the front door when he saw her slowly meandering up the long curved drive, kicking idly at the snow covered ruts and smiling. Smiling the way she used to when she thought no one was looking...a little girl's smile, lopsided and slightly wistful. Nothing like the carefully applied open-mouthed grin that had graced the covers of fashion magazines for three consecutive seasons.

Jenna.

And for one brief instant Cody wanted to call out to her, to shout out her name at the top of his lungs...to scream until the neighbors on both sides would be convinced that Cody Andrews had finally lost his mind.

Instead he leaned against the porch railing and closed his eyes.

Jenna. The way his mind saw her. The raggedy grey pullover bunched at her hips, faded jeans stuffed into cowboy boots, thick auburn hair pushed into the kelly-green watch cap she'd found at a flea-market...

"If your agent saw you looking like that," he'd joke, "she'd burn your contracts and head for the hills!"

And Jenna would strike a familiar pose.

"Why?" She would ask. "Don't you think she'd like my Bag Lady look?"

And they'd laugh together. A million years ago.

When he opened his eyes she was gone.

Hiking the fleece collar up as if trying to protect his thoughts as well as the back of his neck, Cody stepped off the porch and quickly walked down to the rural mailbox at the end of the drive...fighting the urge to look down for footprints he knew weren't there...couldn't be there...

A million years ago. Two million...

He saw her again as he was carrying the mail back to the house. This time she was standing next to the leafless apple tree by the side yard, watching him. The smile was gone.

"Cody?"

The voice was faint but recognizable, and as cold as the frigid morning air.

"Cody?"

This time the voice was behind him, closer... stronger. Cody felt his left leg hit a patch of hidden ice and twist out from under him as he turned.

"Ohmygod! Are you alright, Cody?"

Squinting past the gently swirling flakes, Cody forced a smile to his lips and nodded up at Helen Elliot's substantial down-covered girth.

"Yeah, just demonstrating how graceful ex-running backs can be when we put our minds to it."

The woman knit her brows as she watched him slowly get to his feet. Friends and neighbors for ten years, she had lately taken it upon herself to become his sole provider.

"I didn't mean to startle you, Cody," she said when he finally managed to round up the scattered pile of bills and stand upright. "I just thought you might like some fresh cinnamon rolls."

As he brushed the melting powder off his pants, Cody glanced down at the foil-wrapped baking pan and felt his smile go real.

"You trying to make me fat, Mrs. E?" Stuffing the damp envelopes into his coat pocket he accepted the pan, grumbling good-naturedly. It was still warm and the smell of butter-laden spices cranked up the juice machine in his mouth. "How'm I ever going to make a come-back if you keep doing this to me?"

Helen Elliot chuckled again and tossed her head in a way that might have been becoming in a woman half her age. Both of them knew his talk of a come-back was the biggest joke of all. He was thirty-seven with a knee that could predict storms better than any weather satellite.

And of course there was Jenna...

"Didn't I tell you I like my men chunky?" A blush spread outward from her cold-reddened nose. "Well, anyway, don't let them get cold, okay?"

Cody nodded his head, stealing a sideways glance toward the apple tree. Jenna was still there, leaning across the narrow crotch, waiting for him to finish. It was all he could do to keep his hands steady when he turned around.

"Okay. Thanks Helen."

Her blush deepen at the sound of her first name, creating a ruddy glow that seemed to cover her entire face.

"Y'know, I got a crock pot full of beef stew cookin' right this minute..." She reached out and poked playfully at his ribs. "Like to set it up early so I won't miss my soaps. Anyway, there'll be more than enough..."

She looked past him to the house and Cody felt a shiver worm it's way up his back.

"...How about I send over some for dinner." She refocused on his face. "Save you the trouble of having to cook."

Shit. "I'd love it. Thanks...but I really gotta go now." He lifted the pan as if it were a legitimate alibi. "My goodies are getting cold."

Leering suggestively he added. "All my goodies!"

The blush deepened another fraction of a degree. Pulling the coat tighter around her, the woman brayed at his wit and turned to go. Thank God, Cody thought.

"You're just terrible!" She called back over her shoulder when she reached the end of the drive. "What am I going to do with you?"

"Very little," came a whispered reply.

Spinning on his heel, Cody kept his eyes on the frozen ground until he reached the steps...where he stumbled again. Jenna was perched on the plastic covered porch swing, her legs draw up to her chest, arms wrapped around them. Waiting.

"You're not real," he muttered as he transferred the pan to his left hand and fumbled with the doorknob.

"Cody?"

He twisted his head sharply toward the swing, the words of denial pounding against the back of his throat, only to find the porch empty.

"Jesus."

Taking a deep breath, he pressed his head against the icy door frame and wondered if he was coming down with something. He probably would have stayed in that position for the rest of the morning, his head becoming permanently bonded to the house, sweet-rolls dribbling their cooling juices down the side of his jacket, if he hadn't heard the rhythmic squeak of the swing's rusted coils and the soft, hollow sigh that accompanied it.

The warmth inside the house almost hit him like a physical barrier, drawing out what little strength he still had. Depositing the rolls on the hall table, Cody dug the sodden bills out of the coat's pocket and stared at them. Here, at least, was reality.

Phone, electricity, gas and water...all the nice, neat

little window-envelopes that made you cringe but held no real surprises.

Cody laid them next to the sweet rolls and stared at the envelope remaining in his hand. It was a not-so-nice, not-so-neat monster from the Medical Center, containing the results of Jenna's last battery of tests.

Shivering as if the overburdened furnace had suddenly kicked off, Cody tossed the envelope on top of the others. He didn't have to read it to know what it said...lies with fancy names and price-tags attached to them.

Shrugging out of his coat, Cody picked up the rolls and walked into the kitchen. A couple of minutes in the oven would send the spicy warm scent throughout the house, like an olfactory beacon in the darkness.

Why not? He thought as he set the oven to 350 and shoved the pan in. Smells could sometimes trigger mental responses better than anything else. Didn't the scent of new cut grass bring back memories of first jobs and first dates. One whiff of wood smoke and every adult in the vicinity turned back the clock to a favorite Halloween long past.

So why not the smell of cinnamon rolls? Jenna had loved puttering around the kitchen concocting the most outlandish, calorie-laden desert she could, then beaming at the groaning praise it received. Jenna...who's perfect size ten had kept her a prisoner since adolescence...opening the oven door just a crack and breathing in the wonderfully rich smells.

Jenna...

"Cody, stop it!"

She was standing in the kitchen door, the green watch cap in her hands, her hair glowing like fire in the morning dark house.

"Please, Cody...stop it."

He slammed the oven door harder than he had

intended and fled the room through the narrow dining alcove. Upstairs, a monitor began beeping and he raced toward it, desperate for something concrete to focus on.

Jenna was waiting for him on the first landing,

"...Please, Cody..."

but he managed to get by her without stopping.

The front bedroom, the one they had shared together in another life, was illuminated by the dresser sized life-support system he'd had installed after firing the last nurse.

When questioned, he told the hospital he'd been planning on taking a year sabbatical from the high-school's coaching staff anyway...made up a lie about writing a book on the gross motor structure of adolescent males. He'd made up a different lie for the Savings and Loan when he took out a second mortgage to pay for the device.

He'd gotten used to lying...it was easier than having to listen to so-called friends and experts tell him he was only wasting his time and money prolonging the inevitable.

Cody squeezed his eyes shut and took a deep breath. He couldn't let her see him like this. Swallowing hard, he opened his eyes and forced a smile as he walked toward the bed.

"Hi ya, hon," he whispered, deftly replacing the empty glucose bag with a fresh one before switching off the IV alarm. Readjusting the drip, Cody gave the monitor a quick once-over before returning his attention to the bed.

"How're you feeling this morning?"

Now that the alarm was silent he could hear the soft strains of *Elvira Madigan* playing in the background. Jenna loved Mozart, so Cody had rigged an automatic replay on the tape deck next to the bed to ensured there'd always be music. Occasionally, he'd try to sneak in one of the modern composers like Vangelis for a little variety, but he could tell just by looking at her that she only tolerated them.

And the doctors had the nerve to tell him she was beyond understanding.

"Smell that, baby?" Sniffing loudly, Cody sat down on the side of the bed. "Mrs. E sent over some fresh cinnamon rolls. They must be a thousand calories each, with enough cholesterol to kill every truck driver from here to the turnpike."

Gently he reached out and brushed back the muddy-brown wisps that clung to her forehead. Most of her hair had fallen out after the first round of chemotherapy, but she laughed it off and told her agent that she planned to start a whole new fashion craze...Auschwitz Chic. Five months later, after the poison had circulated itself out of her system, it grew back...the color of dead leaves...and he picked up a bottle of Mumm's to celebrate.

Because she'd licked it.

Had spit in the Ferryman's eye.

Fought for her life and won!

Fifteen months later the cancer invaded her brain.

Game. Set. Match.

"How about I bring you up one later," he asked as he checked the measured flashes that indicated her pulse-rate and oxygen-feed. "Y'know what they say, a little sugar goes a long way."

He pretended the facial tic she'd developed recently was the beginnings of a smile and he nodded. If he soaked the roll in warm water then mashed it he might be able to squeeze a little between her lips. She'd probably enjoy a little change from the liquid diet the abdominal catheter was pumping directly into her. Probably love it.

Being careful not to dislodge the IV needle, Cody picked up her hand and squeezed it gently, ignoring the feel of the knobby bones pressed against his palm.

"We gotta get a little more meat on you, babe. I

know models are supposed to be skinny…but I think you're overdoing it just a little."

He chuckled, remembering the overly-dramatic hysterics she used to indulge in if she gained so much as a half-pound.

"Fat! FAT! I'm getting as big as a pig!"

"A very thin pig," he always answered, "not even suitable for a mini-luau."

And she'd laugh…then throw the nearest pillow. God, he'd give anything to hear her laugh again. "Cody?"

His hand flinched, crushing hers.

"I—It snowed today, honey." He couldn't bring himself to release his grip…to turn and face the other voice.

"Cody, we have to talk."

"First snow. But I don't think it'll stick. Not cold enough."

Cody tried to concentrate on the piano concerto that was playing as a chill crept up his back. He had long ago accepted the rhythmic whirs and hums of the machinery keeping her alive as natural counter-points to the musical scores, but the cold was something else…it didn't belong there. He didn't want to get used to it. Not yet. Not ever, if he could help it.

"Remember when we first moved out here? You'd never lived in snow country before…poor little Californian." The chill deepened. "Jesus, you ran out into it wearing nothing but pajamas…just like a kid. I was sure you were going to catch pneumonia!"

"I remember. You yelled at me all the way back to the house."

"I didn't mean to," he whispered before he could stop himself.

The chill took shape and touched his shoulder.

"Cody…let go."

He looked down at the emaciated woman on the bed and patted her hand softly, feeling the blood rush back into his own fingers as their strangle-hold loosened.

"I can't, babe."

The cold brushed against the side of his face.

"You always were a coward, weren't you Cody? Afraid to face anything that might go against the Great Man's Ideals, huh?"

"NO!"

There was mockery in her voice now, as sharp and cutting as a knife.

"Oh, no? Then I guess you just like keeping me trapped in a rotting carcass. Makes an even better trophy then those stuffed deer heads your drunken buddies hang up over their fireplaces, huh? Tell me, how much you charge them for a look?"

He was on his feet before he knew it, fists balled at his side…the woman on the bed forgotten as he glared at the one standing before him.

"Good," she said, twirling the watch cap around one finger as she nodded. "Anger's one of the easier emotions to deal with. Besides, I always though it made you look even sexier than usual."

Cody felt his legs flutter, threatening at any moment to go out from under him. Jenna. Standing in front of him less than a yard away…and laying in bed…inches away.

He filled his lungs with the humidified air and looked up at the ceiling.

"I'm losing my mind."

"No you're not, Cody."

He tried to laugh, but the sound couldn't get past his lips.

"Oh, yeah. I'm gone." He closed his eyes when he felt her move closer.

"Cody, look at me."

He kept his eyes and mouth closed. Both were an effort.

"It shouldn't be that hard to look at me. After all, you've seen me plenty of times before without make-up." She paused and he heard her sigh. "And it should be a piece of cake after the last couple of months. Or have you gotten to the point where you like your women brainless and drooling?"

Lowering his chin, Cody opened his eyes to find her staring at the bed, the watch-cap bunched into a formless mass between her hands.

"Jenna."

She looked up at the sound of her name and almost smiled. "But you can't be!" He backed up until his hip brushed against the side of the life-support machine. "You're not dead!"

Jenna's grey eyes drifted back to his face. "Aren't I?"

Cody fought down the sudden irrational urge to check the system. If he turned away, even for a second, she might disappear and he didn't want to take that chance. It'd been so long since he'd had a chance to talk to her...

"That's not me, Cody," she said, jerking her head back toward the bed. The autumn-colored hair, still thick and healthy, fell over one shoulder. "It's nothing anymore."

"You're wrong. It's still you!" He swallowed hard when he realized what he was arguing about. And with whom. "Besides, I made you a promise, Jenna, and I can't go back on it."

A small frown formed between her eyes. "Promise?"

Cody took a step forward and reached out to her, but the cold drove him back. Half-turning, he sat on the edge of the bed...between them.

"I promised I'd do everything in my power to keep you alive!" His mouth went dry again. He knew he was losing his mind, there was no other explanation for it, but he couldn't stop. "I promised you it wouldn't end like this."

The frown deepened, etched furrows on her otherwise smooth face.

"But it's already ended, Cody, don't you understand?" Jenna circled the bed until she was opposite him. "The only thing you're keeping alive now is a memory. Please, let me go!"

Without conscious effort, he reached out and touched her hand...her living hand, the one connected to life through the I.V. needle.

"I can't, Jenna. I love you."

"I know." Her voice dropped to a whisper but the frown remained. "Love's a pretty powerful thing...but sometimes it can do more harm than good."

She reached out, as if to touch the body on the bed then shuddered and pulled back.

"You've been holding on to something that doesn't exist anymore. That shouldn't have to exist.

"I want to die now, Cody."

Too much, it was too much. Shaking his head, Cody twisted away from the bed and staggered to his feet...began pacing the narrow distance between the bed and the monitor like a caged animal.

"NO!" He screamed at her. "I won't let you die! I can't..."

Jenna half-smiled, the way she used to whenever he was making an ass of himself, and brushed the hair away from her face.

"You always did have illusions of grandeur, didn't you? Is it fun playing God?" Her mouth twitched upward when she saw the anger flare across his face. "But the truth is that you really aren't doing anything but prolonging the agony. My agony."

Cody dug his elbows into his belly.

"Jenna...I..."

She stepped away from the bed and pulled the watch cap down around her ears.

"I know, but it has to end sometime and it might as well be now. So, how 'bout it, cowboy?" She struck what she once called her High Fashion Hooker stance—legs apart, pelvis out, head tipped back—and winked at him. "Is the little lady worth it?"

His hand touched the machine's control panel and faltered.

Jenna relaxed into a more normal position and shook her head as if she'd read his thoughts. It used to bother Cody when she did that, now it came as a relief.

"No," she whispered. "You'll just be letting go."

He turned away from the bed...from both of them...and mechanically began shutting down the life-support system. He cut the alarm first, afraid that if he heard the frantic beeping he'd react automatically and try to save her. Again.

When the last of the monitor's lines went flat, Cody walked over to the bedside table and turned off the cassette player.

And although he couldn't be sure...would never be sure...in those first few seconds, as the empty house readjusted to the silence, Cody thought he heard her laugh.

YRENA

She looked like a piece of trash someone had tossed to the side of the road. Tiny she was and pale...so, so pale that her skin seemed to glow in the darkness.

At first Konstantin Misurov thought she might not even be real, just some starving sculptor's joke crafted from the late winter snow and draped with rags. Not that it would have surprised him. Since the Great Revolution, Misurov had seen many sculptors starving in the streets of the newly renamed Leningrad. It was only by the greatest luck that he had not joined them; that, and the fact that even a society of equals needed signs to be painted. His talent, once renowned in the Imperial courts, was at least not going to waste.

Ah, she moved...slowly as if the cold had already worked its bony fingers into her, and Misurov blinked away the snow flakes building on his lashes. He'd almost forgotten the child was there and that worried him. It was not like him to indulge in his own misery such that he would let so tender a morsel get away.

Even if he could not paint, life still had its compensations.

The child moved again, drawing her stockinged legs closer to her chest as Misurov closed the distance between them. Her eyes, dark as the rags she wore and betraying the taint of gypsy blood in her veins, raised to the level of his face and stayed there. Even in the shadows

Misurov could see that they held no fear—mistrust, yes...and something else, but not fear.

"Hello, little bird, have you fallen from your nest?"

The child nodded and a ragged seam slipped from her shoulder. Her flesh tone was a subtle mix of cerulean and ash. A less subtle heat filled Misurov's groin an instant before the wind snatched it away.

"You should not be out all alone," he said softly, his breath steaming in the cold. "Aren't you afraid?"

As he crouched on the hard packed snow in front of her, Misurov was aware of the others who shared the night with them. They were huddled forms...vague, faceless shadows...background images filling in an unfinished landscape. But one never knew in times like these what a mere shadow might remember, or a background image report to the wolfish authorities.

A lifetime ago, before the revolution, Misurov had relied upon his position in the old regime to make his "indiscretions" invisible. Now they would make him just another target for re-education.

"Where is your mother, little bird?" he asked gently, in a voice as soft as velvet.

Something glistened in the corner of her eye, just for a moment, then it was gone. A tear? Misurov wondered.

"Ah," he said, leaning forward over the woolen patches on the knees of his trousers, "you are alone."

She nodded again and an ebony lock slipped from beneath the shawl she wore over her head. Slowly, as if he were trying to pet a feral cat, Misurov reached out a gloved hand. He could feel the coldness of her cheek even through the layer of greased wool. Poor frozen little thing.

"I am Konstantin Ilitch Misurov" he said through the swirling steam of his breath, "I was once a great artist with many friends, but now I too am alone in this world."

She seemed unimpressed. Misurov sighed and watched his breath encircle the child's head like a holy aura. Almost immediately an image appeared on the empty canvas he kept behind his eyelids: A gypsy Madonna huddling before the Angel of the Lord.

A dirty, half-starved gypsy Madonna.

Misurov felt the ice in his beard crack as he smiled. What a typical bourgeois thought, he reminded himself. But what a painting it would have made. Ah, well.

"What is your name, child?"

The dark eyes left his face, glancing quickly to the left and right, a slight frown creasing the smoothness of her brow. Was his little Madonna looking for help or simply making sure that whatever proposition he was about to offer met no opposition? Bourgeois or not, Misurov prayed it was the latter. It would make things so much simpler if she knew the ways of the world and men. The innocent tended to scream and claw when he dragged them away.

"My name is Yrena. Vojvoda."

Her voice was as brittle as the cold and just as numbing. No trace of her breath moved through the darkness. She must be all but frozen.

"My mother's name was Yrena," Misurov lied. Again. He had given his mother so many names throughout the years that he no longer remembered what it really was. Part of him hoped it'd been Yrena. "But Vojvoda? That's the name of a village, isn't it? Is that where you come from?"

She stared at him without answering. Did it matter? No.

"Are you hungry, Yrena?"

YES! He could see it in her eyes, the way her body tensed. Of course she was hungry, most of Russia…no, most of the Union of Soviet Socialist Republics was hungry.

Nodding, Misurov dropped his hand to her bare

shoulder and squeezed gently. Her flesh was as hard and unyielding as polished marble.

"Come then," he said, pulling the child to her feet as he stood, "I don't live far."

They walked slowly, the loose rags covering the child's feet leaving serpentine tracks in the snow behind them, only Misurov's breath steaming the air.

Yrena was so quiet that he kept looking down the long, black line of his great-coat sleeve to make sure she was still there. She was—a silent shadow at his side…his own tiny piece of night to caress and bury himself in.

The thought kept Misurov warm.

She had wrapped the scarf across her face so that only her dark eyes showed, twin holes punched into the white canvas of her flesh. And she never blinked, his little Yrena Vojvoda…his little girl who named herself for a village that might not even exist anymore. His little child of the night—never looking up at him, never questioning him about their destination. Silent and servile. The way he preferred them.

When another night traveler suddenly appeared in front of them, its gender and purpose disguised by the layers of snow and clothing it wore, Misurov tightened his grip on the child's shoulder. But only he trembled.

Yrena continued walking at his side, as indifferent to his touch as she was to the cold and darkness.

Two long blocks down and one across, and Misurov pointed to a narrow garret set above an empty stable. He was lucky to have found the place, with so many going without. The walls were thick and sturdy, the floors solid enough, and the one window faced north. Even the rats, poor thin things, were a source of comfort. They made him not feel so alone.

Misurov paused for a moment and studied the

weathered lines of his current home, nodding. Whatever it had been before, it made a passable artist's studio.

Or at least it would have if he were still an artist.

The ice tugged at the hairs in Misurov's beard as he threw back his head and laughed, his breath a white plume billowing into the night sky. It was such a good joke, such a terrible good joke to play on a man who had once lived only to create worlds with pigment and brush. Ah, God.

A gentle tug on the hem of his sleeve brought Misurov back.

Looking down, he met Yrena's eyes and nodded.

"I am not as much a madman as I appear, little bird," he said, releasing his grip on her shoulder to take her hand. "Don't be afraid."

"I'm not," came the muffled reply.

Thanking whatever angel or saint it was that had managed to escape detection by the new government in order to place such a child in his hands, Misurov pulled her close and began walking them toward the narrow wooden stair-case that led to the garret. One of the other misplaced denizens of the area was singing, accompanied by a bandura—a sad song, probably gypsy or Ukrainian…definitely anti-revolutionary. The rich baritone rolled through the frozen darkness, bringing with it memories of palace life— of golden children with satin skin and virgin canvases to fill with the finest Parisian tinctures, and where the light of a thousand candles was captured and reflected by snowflakes created by Faberge' instead of God.

Misurov shook the frozen tears away from his eyes. Foolish man, he chided himself, those things are gone forever. Dead.

"Let's hurry and get inside," he whispered, half-tugging, half-carrying the child up the stairs. "It's cold and you are hungry."

"Yes," she said, "starving."

Her voice was so pitiful it almost melted Misurov's heart. Almost. But not quite.

The brass hasp screeched as he opened the door, inciting a rolling tide of squeals from the rats as Misurov stepped inside. His palatial estate occupied a space no bigger than a pony-stall in the Czar's stables and was as frigid as a grave. Another chorus of angry squeals met his blind fumblings for the wall shelf next to the door where he kept a tallow candle and matches. A thump followed by a high pitched grunt let him know that the rats had again found a way up to the shelf.

Misurov felt a thumb-size strip gnawed out of the middle of the candle when he picked it up; the empty paint pot he kept the dozen or so matches in had been upended, the precious contents scattered or eaten. It took him another three pats along the shelf before the sodden fingers of his glove found a single match.

"Damn vermin," he growled, igniting the sulfur along the underside of the shelf. Shadows danced along the empty walls as he fought chills to light the candle. "If this new government of ours really wanted to do something, they would classify rats along with other political dissidents and send them all to Siberia. Bah…but enough of things we cannot change, isn't that so, Yrena?"

Silence and darkness answered him.

Misurov tottered slightly as he turned, the narrow, rat-chewed candle quivering. Shadows fled across the walls, solidifying finally into the tiny figure still standing in the open doorway. Perhaps fear had found her at last.

"Yrena."

She didn't move—How many times had he told his models not to move?—didn't lower her dark eyes from his, the pinprick of light they reflected the only things moving.

"What is it, Yrena?" Misurov asked softly, his voice a lullaby, "I won't hurt you. Come in, there is nothing to be afraid of."

Her body started moving forward at the word "come". And by the time the last echo of the last word died Misurov found himself being grasped around the waist in a surprisingly strong bear-hug.

Misurov's laughter clouded the air as he swung her up to his chest and slammed the door with a kick. She didn't seem to notice when he released his hold just long enough to slide the iron inner bolt shut. His quiet little bird didn't even seem to notice when he carried her to the tiny stone fireplace four paces away and set her before it.

A half-dozen thrusts with the fire-iron into the bed of coals and a ruddy glow filled the room, exposing piles of dust covered canvases propped up against the walls. In recent years they had proven to be a better source of fuel than a lasting monument to his genius.

To prove that, Misurov grabbed a painting from the stack nearest the hearth and set it on the embers. The portrait, showing one of the Czar's brood mares, sizzled into flames almost instantly, the heat from it sending shivers down Misurov's back. "There now," he said, laying the poker aside to rub his hands vigorously in the warmth, "isn't that better?"

Than what? Yrena's dark eyes asked silently.

Another shiver raced through him. Sighing, Misurov pulled one of the only two chairs he owned near the fire and let the wet coat slip from his shoulders. Wisps of steam that smelled like wet dogs curled up from the material.

"Come, then," he said, gently pulling the shawl away from her face and fingering one of the ebony locks it exposed, "off with those wet things before you catch your death."

Misurov felt his hands tremble, but not from the cold.

"We'll get you warm and dry first," he said, putting a promise into his voice, "and then food."

With that one word, Misurov saw more emotion in the child's face than he had since meeting her. Her need tore at his heart, but it didn't stop him from undressing her. If he could no longer paint, then life owed him some sort of compensation.

Without her shawl, dress and stockings, Yrena was little more than blued flesh and knobby bones; barely a mouthful.

But beggars cannot be choosers, Konstantin, he reminded himself as he reached down to slip the child's gray undershift from her shoulders. And you most certainly have become a beggar in this—

Misurov was still chiding fate when Yrena lunged forward and sank her teeth into his wrist. The pain made him react without thinking, backhanding her to the floor, her shift coming away in his hand.

Blood dripping from the jagged wound at his wrist.

She lay naked at his feet, but for the first time in his life Misurov didn't care.

"You little bitch," he screamed, his right boot was already cocked and waiting to spring, "why the hell did...you...do...?"

Misurov's anger and shock transformed, scattered like ash borne before the winds as he gazed into Yrena's dark eyes. The hunger that lurked there was a living creature that reached out to him the way he had once reached out for the tender flesh of children. He felt it close around his soul. Pulling him. Luring him into its depths.

Without any effort on his part, Misurov kneeled before her and held out his bloodied arm. The dark eyes shifted to the wound, a sardonic grin slowly parting her lips. The light from the burning portrait reflecting off strong, white fangs.

"Papa," she whispered, reaching up to take Misurov's hand. "Papa."

As Yrena's teeth pierced his flesh a second time an ecstasy Misurov had never found even in the arms of children exploded in his soul, creating images in his mind so real, so sublime that he began painting them on the invisible canvas of air around him.

Yrena...his little bird...his little gypsy Madonna encircled by the ruby-red light of Heaven as she—

The sound of retching shattered the illusion and Misurov collapsed, tumbling hard to the rough wooden floor.

"What the—?"

Yrena was curled into a ball, hunched over her knees, the ridges of her backbone writhing snake-like beneath the thin layer of skin as she vomited. It took Misurov a moment to realize what she was throwing up was blood. His blood.

"God, protect me," he prayed, forgetting that God had been declared dead as he scrambled away from her; stopping only when his own spine collided with the paintings laying against the wall behind him. "What are you?"

She looked up, his little bird, tears the color of garnets leaving tracks against her snow colored cheeks—her fangs, like ivory scimitars, stained with his blood.

"You're not my Papa," she whimpered, "and I'm so hungry."

His little bird. His little Madonna.

A verdalak!

Misurov crossed himself quickly, forgetting again as he pressed his knuckles against the front of his teeth in place of the ceremonial kiss and watched the child slowly lower her head back to the blood spattered floor.

No wonder she was alone. And starving. If the legends his Baba told him as a child were true, the verdalak was that form of vampire which could feed only on members of its own family.

"My God," he whispered, louder...and louder, pounding his fist against the floor. "My God. My God."

And God answered.

It was at that instant the frame within the fire cracked and spit out a smoldering piece of itself next to his hand. He could still see the intricate carving that had once decorated the wood, reduced now to charcoal...nothing... useless...a shadow of what it had been.

Like Yrena. Like his little bird.

Like himself...nothing...useless...

A painting appeared in his mind: Yrena lying there, cowering, night shadow and firelight playing over the contours of her naked body.

Yrena.

Misurov's fingers stung from the heat of the charcoal sliver as he sketched the outline. The floor was too rough for fine detail, too worn for the delicate features that soon appeared.

"Yrena. Lift your head and look at me...no, too much. Lower your chin. To the left, move your chin to the left, you're throwing a shadow across your arm. Yes...that's it. That's it."

A moment later two Yrenas stared questioningly back at him—one, the reanimated corpse, hunger filling its empty eyes; the other, a perfect Madonna surrounded by light.

Yes.

Nodding, Misurov stood and grabbed another canvas from the pile behind him. The painting was of a stately young woman in a flowing white gown—a lady of the court or perhaps even one of the Grand Duchesses themselves—walking along a Spring path, golden sun dappling her amber hair, pink cherry blossoms cascading about her.

It was soulless. Dead. As imaginative as the signs he now painted.

A thin cloud of dust trailed across the room as he carried it to the long abandoned easel sitting beneath the room's window. The remains of a silken shirt, dust stained and torn and yellowed with age, hung from the point of the skeletal frame like a decaying corpse. Misurov had placed it there in hopes of hiding one piece of the past with another. Fool, he chided himself as it tossed it over his shoulder, fitting the painted canvas into the frame.

A tube of gesso that had been in the tray for God know's how long fell when he moved the easel closer to the fire and shattered. Misurov crushed the hardened plaster flakes beneath his boots. It didn't matter. He could still paint her even without preparing the canvas. He could still paint.

Misurov looked at the monster-child over the edge of the canvas and felt something stir in his belly…his own buried dead rising from their coffins to feast on his life's blood.

Like Yrena.

The charcoal swept across the painting, obliterating one image as it created another. And Yrena watched as complacent and silent as stone, only her dark eyes breaking the illusion as they darted left and right, following the blood on his wrist.

"Here," he said, bringing the wound to his face so her eyes would follow. "Look at me here."

"I'm hungry."

Misurov nodded and quickly sketched in the eyes before they broke contact.

"Of that I have no doubt, verdalak," he said, softening the shadows caressing the charcoal face with the side of his hand. "How long did it take you to kill your family? A month? Two? Not even wolves eat their own kind."

A garnet tear blossomed in the corner of one eye. Misurov copied it in charcoal, mentally keeping a list of the colors he'd have to buy to finish the painting.

"But I couldn't help it," she whined—a little girl being chastised for some minor misdoing. "My brother Oleg…"

"Ah, your brother," Misurov said, deepening the look of anguish in the thin lips. "Is he here in the city with you?"

"No."

Bold strokes—three, four, five—and ebony curls encircled her unpainted face.

"There is no one left then?"

The garnet tear fell. "No."

"So you decided to come to the big city, huh? Walked all the way from Vojvoda to see if there was some long forgotten family member…like a wolf cub tracking lambs. But it wasn't that easy, was it, little bird?"

Misurov let the charcoal drop from his fingers as he took a step back to look at the sketch. Yrena, like the child Madonna, stared calmly back at him. Where there had been only need and hunger, there was now acceptance. Where there had only been shadow, there was now light.

"You came all that way and you found nothing." Misurov reached out and brushed his fingers lightly over the charcoaled shoulders. "Well, you are in good company…even the living have found nothing here."

"But I'm so hungry," the creature moaned, the points of her fangs digging into her colorless bottom lip.

Misurov nodded, understanding. "As I was."

Absently rubbing the charcoal into his beard, he walked back to her and kneeled—slowly pulled the blood soaked cuff away his wrist and held it out. Yrena yelped like a booted hound, covering her face with bloodied fingers.

"Go away," she whimpered, "leave me alone."

How many other children had told him that? Fifty? One hundred? And how many times had he heeded that plea? Not once. Then or now.

"Shush, little bird," Misurov said as softly as he had every other time, "I'm not going to hurt you. Look, see what I have for you?" Dark eyes lifted just enough to gaze at the wound. "Come, my Yrena, eat."

Caution, like black ice forming across the surface of a pond, momentarily replaced the hunger in her eyes. In the flickering light, Misurov watched the muscles in her narrow thighs and calves quiver.

"Why are you doing this?" she hissed. "Why aren't you afraid of me?"

Why? Why wasn't he?

The joints in his knees popped as he kneeled next to her. Why? Turning his head, Misurov studied the sketch he'd just done. It had been so long since anything had stirred him enough to go back to his easel…so very long since he'd felt truly alive.

"Because," Misurov said, on his knees now, moving his bloodied wrist closer even as she backed away, "I need you to model for me."

"But I can't," she whimpered, "I can only feed on…I can only…"

Her sobs sounded human enough.

"I know, I know," Misurov said, taking both her cold hands in his. "But listen to me, little bird, there is a way. I can adopt you. Do you understand? I do adopt you. That makes me your Papa now. Understand?"

The skin around Yrena's mouth tightened. She understood.

"My Papa."

"Yes."

"My Papa."

Misurov felt his body jerk as she darted forward, her fangs golden in the firelight and glistening with drool. It was all he could do to keep her at bay, the wound at his wrist held just out of reach.

"Yes, but listen to me, verdalak," he commanded, "I will be your Papa but you will not feed off of me. I have many cousins in this city, many more than any family needs, and each night I will tell you where to find one. You may drain that one to the dregs, I don't care, but then you will come back to me. Only to me, do you understand that?"

Yrena nodded, less child and more monster as she nuzzled the wound and whined.

"All right then, you may take just a little...to seal our bargain, so to speak. AH, GOD!"

Light and fire coursed through Misurov when she reopened the wound and began to lap, her slug-white tongue making kitten sounds in the stillness. Closing his eyes, Misurov shuttered and saw colors swirl into a hundred paintings...masterpieces that had yet to be created. Hundreds? No...thousands and all of Yrena. All of them of his little bird.

Misurov arched his back, groaning at the strength of the spasm that rocked through him.

God, it was good to be painting again.

***

He loved her.

Not the way he had once feigned love with living

children, using their bodies to fill an emptiness he'd never even known existed until Yrena came into his life.

Because she had given him back his life and filled it the way her painted image filled the walls of his room. His little bird, gazing back at him regardless of where he looked—but always in shadows, features highlighted only by candle light, the colors muted…dark.

She required so little of the spectrum: Black, mulberry, lapis and cerulean, alabaster and ivory for her flesh, a touch of mustard and primrose for the candle's wan glow, and vermillion for her lips and cheeks.

It was sad in a way, Misurov mused as he swirled a drop of red into black, now that he had money enough to buy every hue ever imagined.

One of the benefits of Yrena's nightly "family visits" was the presents she brought home to her loving Papa. Sometimes rubles and sometimes things that could be more discreetly bartered for the supplies he needed. His lovely little bird.

Misurov felt no remorse. His morally superior family had kept their disapproval of him a secret as long as he was their link to court; but almost at the same moment the Czar and his family were falling beneath a summer rain of bullets, Misurov's was denouncing him to anyone who would listen as a pervert and Menshevick.

Bastards.

Rolling his shoulders against the cramp that had worked its way into them, Misurov stuck the sable-tipped brush between his teeth and took a step back…nodding at the Yrena that stared back at him from the finished canvas.

She was standing half hidden by the open door, looking back into the room over her right shoulder…the faintest hint of a smile playing at the corners of her mouth.

It was that smile which had driven Misurov back to

the easel, the first real smile he had ever seen from her. The first, he prayed, of many more to come.

Misurov heard her light step on the stairs only a moment before she opened the door.

"I'm home, Papa," she said, closing the door and walking quickly to his side, her woolen cape fluttering behind her like angel wings.

Smiling around the brush, Misurov leaned forward to received her offered kiss. And felt a shiver nettle his spine. Her lips were icicles against his flesh, her breath the wind from a slaughter house.

His little love.

"Did you remember to do as I told you, Yrena?" He asked as he took the brush from between his teeth, then tossed both it and the palette to the floor. He had asked that same question for twenty-six nights in a row.

"Yes. Papa."

"And there was no trouble?"

"No. Papa."

She was such a good child.

"Come then and tell your Papa all about it."

Misurov flexed the stiffness from his fingers as he walked to the hearth. The roaring fire he had started before beginning to paint had reduced itself to a fist-sized mound of rolling coals. Where did the time go? Picking up the wrought iron poker he stabbed the embers and watched a million sparks fly to heaven.

When he turned around she was standing at his side, the knife blade laid out across both palms. Even though he didn't think the taint of the verdalak would extend to Yrena's "adopted family", Misurov didn't believe in taking chances. Instead of using her fangs, he had instructed his beloved child to slit throats or wrists to feed.

What news there'd been on the streets had been full

of the ghastly murders. The work of a madman, it was thought, or a Loyalist out to avenge the Empire.

Fools, Misurov thought as he curled his fingers around the knife handle and brought it into the light. As usual it had been licked clean. Misurov nodded.

"Well, then," he said, listening to the rustle of her clothing whisper through the gloom behind him, "what have you brought your Papa tonight?"

There was no answer.

Misurov turned to find her staring at her newest portrait. There wasn't a trace of the earlier smile on her florid lips.

"Do you like it?" he asked.

"No," she said. "Papa."

"But why not, my little love?"

Her eyes traced the lines of the panting. "Because it's like a mirror," she said. "They all are. Do you hate me that much. Papa?"

"Hate you?" The knife slipped from Misurov's hand, clattering hollowly against the hearth stone as he stood. "How can you say such a thing? Just look around you, Yrena…these paintings…"

Misurov took a step toward her and spread his arms to the room. Smiled at each image he had made of her.

"These paintings tell how much I love you. Look here. And here, look." Misurov spun on the heels of his boots, stopping when he faced the first portrait he'd ever done of her, the night she had come into his life—laying naked before the fire, the soulless eyes glaring back at him. "You are my reason to live, Yrena, my reason to paint. How could I not love you? My God, how could you say such a thing?"

She shrugged. It was so human, so child-like an action that Misurov chuckled.

Until she turned and stared at him.

"What?" he asked. "What is it, my little bird?"

"That was the last one, wasn't it. Papa?"

Misurov made it all the way to his chair by the hearth before his legs gave out from under him.

Something scraped beneath the heel of his boot. Looking down he saw the knife blade gleam like blood in the embers' glow. Like blood. A grinding ache shot through Misurov's back and shoulders as he leaned forward to pick it up.

"I don't know what you mean, little bi—"

"You don't have any more family left. Do you. Papa?"

Misurov stared at his elongated features—blood red—in the blade.

"No. How did you know?"

"This one was so old and thin, not even much juice left, like the last apple in a barrel. Papa."

Misurov nodded, watched his reflection shimmer.

"Do you hate me, Yrena?"

"No," she answered from across the room. "Papa."

"Do you love me?"

"No. Papa."

"Are you going to leave me?"

"Yes. Papa."

Letting his eyes gaze at the portraits surrounding him, Misurov lifted the knife and pressed the point of the blade into the throbbing vein at the side of his neck. There was less pain than he hoped for.

"Well, then," he said, "show your Papa what you have brought him before you go."

Misurov heard the rustle of her cape and the tap, tap, tap of her boots crossing the room toward him. But already she sounded so very far away.

"Here. Papa."

The goblet was exquisite, turned smoky quartz crystal with a reeded gold base, just the sort of thing his late spinster cousin would keep. A ghost from the past.

Like his paintings.

Like Yrena.

"How fitting," he said, holding the goblet up to catch the blood oozing from his throat.

She took the first brimming goblet full and drained it dry.

He filled it a second time. A third. It was getting harder to talk, to think.

"Will you love me when I'm dead, Yrena?"

"No," she said, licking her lips. "Papa."

Misurov heard glass break as Yrena climbed onto his lap and began kissing his neck. Closing his eyes, Misurov watched the colors fade from dull gray to black to blood red.

"...JUST A LITTLE BUG..."

"You almost ready?"

Kate stood in the doorway and felt her fingers dig into the thin, summer-weight sweatshirt she was carrying. She never understood why they kept hospitals so cold.

Like walking into a tomb.

The memory of standing next to her father's hospital bed (watching him die) shivered its way up her spine.

NO! She wouldn't think about that. Not now. Not ever. Because this wasn't the same thing. This time the doctors were wrong. This time it wasn't her father slipping away. This time it was her baby and the doctors were wrong.

Kate let go of the air that somehow managed to get trapped in her lungs and smiled. She looks better today, Kate reassured herself—just like she'd done every morning for the last six months. Stronger. Healthier.

She DOES, dammit.

"Do I gotta go?"

Kate blinked and found herself looking into eyes that were too old and worn out to belong to a nine year old child. It's just the drugs, Kate reminded herself as she walked into the sweet/sour/medicine smell of the room.

The sick room.

Her daughter's room.

Carrie Marie McCarthy's room.

Carrie and Kate.

The McCarthy Girls: Stronger than week old garlic pizza, faster than a speeding skateboard, able to leap insurmountable obstacles with just a blinding smile and the toss of strawberry-blond curls.

Except Carrie's curls had been the first victim of the Chemotherapy war she'd been consigned to. The slightly crooked smile, that once reminded Kate so much of herself, had been the second.

But it was just the drugs.

"Well, of course you have to go, silly," Kate said, trying not to breathe the sick smell in. Trying to keep the smile fastened to her lips.

Trying to pretend everything was going to be fine.

Trying.

"What would Dr. John say if his most favorite girlfriend in the whole world didn't show up for her appointment?"

The pale, almost colorless eyes rolled beneath the floppy "hippie" hat they'd found the day the last of her hair fell out. "He'd be happy," Carrie whispered, her voice almost lost in the soft, constant hiss from the oxygen tube strapped to her face. "That way he wouldn't have to see me die."

Kate's nails dug through the material and found the skin on her forearm—left four burning scratches before she forced herself to laugh.

Forced. As if the bright pink-and-white, stuffed animal cluttered, disinfected, oxygen-rich, sick-smell room was only a set from some prime time Sit-Com and she was laughing on cue.

Right before the commercial break.

"Now you really are being silly, Carrot-cake," she said as she walked toward the bed. "You're not going to die." You're not, you're not, you're NOT! "You just have a little bug. Dr. John told you that, remember?"

"You have a bug inside you," the tall, silver-haired man had told Carrie, scrunching almost in half as he took both her tiny hands in his one and smiled. "Just a little bug that we're going to SWAT, okay?"

And Carrie had giggled and tossed her red-gold curls and asked if she was going to have to swallow a fly-swatter.

But then the giggles stopped.

And never came back.

Just a bug, they told her…like the "flu bugs" and "cold bugs" Kate used to make out of paper bags stuffed with newspaper…

Just a bug…because telling a child she had cancer was too scary.

It didn't matter if the parents were so scared one of them ran away instead of facing it. And the other one kept forcing herself to laugh.

And pretend. That it really was only a bug.

"I can feel it."

Kate blinked her eyes as if she was waking up (trying to wake up) from a bad dream.

"What?"

Carrie looked up and gently touched the center of her narrow chest where the tumor lay, growing like a misplaced embryo. Kate had finally let herself look at the last series of X-rays—had finally seen the malignant shadow that was eating her baby.

Alive.

"I can feel the bug," Carrie whispered, looking serious. Looking old. "I can feel it moving."

Kate swallowed the lump that had formed in her own throat and took too deep a breath. Smelled the odor of disinfectant and medicines and death that hovered in the room.

"Carrie, I want you to listen to me, okay? You...you can't feel the bug because it's —" Too far inside you. "— it's just a little teenie-weenie, little thing."

Carrie's lower lip inched into a pout.

"No it's not, Mom. Not any more."

Oh GOD! "All right, that's enough. I don't want to hear any more about the bug, okay?" Kate let her voice drift into a *this is it and I mean it* tone as she held out the sweatshirt. "Now, hurry up and put this on, Dr. John's waiting."

"But it really is moving, Mom." Tears welled almost instantly. "Honest, Momma. Here...feel it."

Kate had been able to avoid touching her daughter except for the necessary cleaning and dressing and perfunctory bedtime kiss—until now—because she didn't want to feel how little of her daughter the bug had left.

"Carrot-cake," she pleaded, "I promise I'll...touch the bug later, but right now we have to—"

"Please? Momma."

Dammit.

Letting the weight of the sweatshirt pull her down, Kate sat on the edge of the Aladdin bedspread and laid her palm over the matching cartoon on the front of her daughter's tee-shirt. She kept it there just long enough to feel the faint, rhythmic struggling of Carrie's heart.

"Do you feel it, mom?"

Please feel it, her eyes said, *please feel the bug.*

Kate pulled her hand back quickly—fingers spread, palm up—and gaped at it. As if she really had felt the bug.

"It tickled," she lied. Kept lying in whispered, secret tones so the bug wouldn't hear. "And you know something, Carrot-cake? I think it's getting smaller."

A look that was almost the old Carrie—wide eyes and crooked smile—blossomed for an instant. And was gone almost as quickly.

"Nah uh…the bug's getting bigger and it's moving all the time now, like it can't get comfortable." A single tear finally worked its way out of Carrie's eye and into the hollow of her cheek. "It feels…funny. I wish it would just go away."

Oh God, so do I.

Kate pressed her hand back against her daughter's chest and felt the overworked lungs labor despite the constant stream of oxygen. And nodded.

Another lie wouldn't hurt.

Not now.

"It will, baby," she said. "Y'know, I just had another thought…maybe the bug knows Dr. John is getting ready to swat it. Maybe it's packing up its bug bags right now. Maybe it's scared."

Kate was going to embellish the tale a little more when something twisted lazily beneath her hand.

"I don't think so, momma," Carrie said, as Kate pulled her hand slowly away. "I don't think it's scared of anything."

***

"A what?"

Kate brushed her hair out of her eyes and almost laughed out loud. Would have if they weren't standing in the Waiting Room filled with dying children and their already grieving parents. Dying children…but not hers…not Carrie.

"A bug, Dr. John, a real bug…or something alive." Kate pressed her hand against the elderly doctor's white lab coat. "Right here. I felt it move Dr. John and tumors don't move. So it has to be something else, right? So maybe it's something that you can remove!"

Kate saw her reflection in the doctor's glasses as he

stepped closer and placed both his hands over her one…the same way he'd held Carrie's hands when he told her the lie about having just a little bug.

But it WASN'T a lie! Kate wanted to scream. It really IS a "bug" of some kind. I felt it move. I felt it! I felt it!

"If you felt anything at all," the doctor said softly, "it was probably an air bubble beneath the skin. There's no bug, real or sugar coated. I've just seen the last series of X-rays, Kate…the cancer's metastasized. There's nothing more we can do."

***

Nothing more we can do

Nothing more

nothing

Kate hit the horn hard enough to deepen the heat-crack in its plastic housing and cursed.

Silently.

There was more than enough noise already.

The city sounds poured in through the open windows and fought with a stereo that had been cranked up high to compensate. But Kate could still hear her.

Carrie.

Laying across the back seat and puking into the Halloween Happy Meal bucket she'd gotten last year.

B.C. Before Cancer.

Kate hit the horn again and saw dark eyes glare at her from the rear view mirror in the truck ahead. Dammit! If there was nothing more they could do then why did they still give her the Chemo?

And why did they tell her to just take Carrie home when she was supposed to stay at the hospital—in a nice, air conditioned room with crisp sheets and around-the-clock

nurses and cool metal bowls she could puke her guts out into
so Kate could have a night off.

Away from the cancer.

But it moved.

Kate tightened her grip on the sweat-slick steering
wheel and maneuvered the car over another half yard of
steaming asphalt.

Carrie was supposed to have stayed in the hospital
for observation because they were going to try "something
new". That's what Dr. John had told them both.

The last time.

This time he had stayed with Carrie throughout the
therapy—stroking her thin hands and talking softly...so
softly that Kate hadn't been able to hear what he was saying.
But Carrie had nodded. Solemnly. A little old lady in a floppy hat and cartoon sweatshirt.

This time, after Dr. John told her there was nothing
more they could do for her child, he'd hugged Kate and
slipped a pill bottle into her hand, saying—

Kate pressed her back against the damp upholstery
and crooked her elbow out the window, yelping when the hot
metal seared her flesh.

"You okay, Momma?"

Carrie'd heard, even above the noise and nausea.
God, what else had she heard? Her mother screaming at the
doctor that the thing inside her...the thing killing her really
was some kind of bug?

Kate pulled her arm back into the car and tapped
the accelerator—moved the car another quarter of a foot.

"Yeah, baby. I'm fine." She glanced into the rear-
view mirror even though she knew Carrie wouldn't have the
strength to sit up. "How're you doing?"

The sound of dry retching answered her.

Kate let her eyes shift down to her purse, thinking

that if she stared hard enough she'd be able to see the small amber bottle with its single white tablet.

—saying, "She's put up one hell of a fight, Kate, but her little body's just about worn out. You know I can't tell you to do this…but it might be easier on both of you—her especially—if she just went to sleep."

To sleep.

Like it would be so easy.

The car jerked and stalled as Kate panic-stopped a few inches off the truck's bumper. God, that's all she needed. Even a minor fender-bender would be more than she could stand.

Taking a deep breath of the exhaust-flavored air, Kate braced her arms and restarted the car. She had to get Carrie home.

To bed.

to sleep

Kate put the car in gear and let the traffic drag them along. A half block away from where she stalled, Kate leaned over and turned the stereo still higher—trying to drown out the lullabies that had begun playing in her head.

***

"Can I get you something, baby? A pop-cicle? I've got cherry…your favorite."

Kate felt the cool breeze from the swamp cooler licking the sweat off her back as she waited for an answer. They'd moved the air-conditioner into Carrie's room right after her first "bug-swatting session"…because the "bug juice" had made her skin feel like it was on fire.

But even then, as sick as she was, Carrie had made Kate promise they'd move it back to the front room just as soon as she got better.

Just as soon as the bug got swatted.

Once upon a time.

"Carrot-cake? Are you asleep?"

The oxygen-tube hissed...but that was all; and a new, colder chill raced up Kate's spine. Freezing her solid. Making her tip-toe to the bed instead of running.

Making her whisper instead of screaming.

"Baby?"

Carrie was laying on her side, her tiny body almost lost in the Hard Rock Cafe tee/night shirt she was wearing, curled around the threadbare teddy that had been her constant companion since birth, one arm bent toward her head—blue-tipped fingers absently making circles on her bare scalp the way they once had made red-gold ringlets.

"The bug's too big, Momma," she said slowly... carefully...the way she once did when working out a really hard math problem. "That's what Dr. John said. He said it's too big and now there's no room left for me."

Kate's own heart felt like it stopped beating then. "No, baby, Dr. John was just fooling around ..."

"Nah uh."

Carrie dropped her hand to the stuffed toy and hugged it to her chest—pressed it hard against the spot where the "bug" had gotten too big.

Kate managed to make it to the edge of the bed before her legs went out from under her. She hoped Carrie couldn't see how her hand was shaking as she reached out and touched the bear. The one and only "class" Kate had attended at the hospital, had recommended that the "Caregiver" (her—the living) tell the "Short Termer" (Carrie—the dying) when it became clear that their "departure" (death) was imminent.

So they could prepare themselves.

As if they were only going away on a trip.

Bye-bye…write when you get there. Have fun.

But no one had been able to tell Kate what the "Care-giver" was supposed to do once the train had pulled out of the station.

"Carrie…honey, listen to me." Kate scooted up until she felt her daughter's bony knees jab her thigh. "Dr. John doesn't know everything! There are a lot of other doctors we can see. Or maybe we can go get an exterminator."

She'd wanted to make the last part a joke, but her voice had cracked and almost strangled her.

Carrie hadn't noticed.

"What's it like to die, momma?"

Kate squeezed her eyes shut and shook her head. No! NO! I'm not ready for this. Not yet…Please God…not YET!

"You think the bug'll die?"

Carrie was staring straight ahead when Kate opened her eyes.

"I hope it doesn't," she said, easing her grip on the teddy bear. "It wouldn't be fair if the bug died, too. Would it, Momma?"

Kate reached past the teddy bear and touched the spot just above Carrie's heart. It was just a little bug…but if it died there wouldn't be anything left …

"No," she said, "it wouldn't."

When Carrie closed her eyes, Kate stood up and balled her hands into fist. No, it wouldn't be fair…but NOTHING was fair anymore. Part of her wanted to scream and pound the walls at the unfairness of it, but all she had the strength to do was stand there and watch her daughter's life shut itself off.

Knowing there was not a damned thing she could do about it.

Except make it easier.

"Momma'll be right back, baby."

Kate didn't stop to think…didn't stop moving until her fingers found the pill bottle in her purse and closed around it. Then she stopped. And looked down. And thought about what she was doing and about all the things they would never do—had never done—and dropped the bottle back into her purse.

"No."

Failure only happened when you gave up…and there were still plenty of things she could do. Hundreds of other doctors who might help. Experimental treatments that could—

Kate spun around, gasping at the sound of shattering glass. Oh, God.

Images of Carrie laying on the floor like a broken doll…neck twisted, suffocating, knowing only agony in the last moments of her life…flooded Kate's mind as she ran back to the room.

"CARRIE!"

The silence seemed louder than the steady hum of the swamp cooler. Louder even than the sound a sliver of glass made when it suddenly came loose and shattered against the top of the cooler, sprinkling down over the other shards from the broken window like frozen rain.

Kate leaned against the door frame and stared at the discarded thing that lay crumpled on Carrie's bed.

It lay on its back. The paper-thin remains of one arm still curled around the old teddy bear, the Hard Rock tee mercifully thrown back over the face. As Kate watched, the transparent skin that surrounded the bloodless rent where Carrie's chest had been began to fold in on itself and harden.

Like a cocoon drying out after the butterfly has left.

A cocoon.

It was just a bug after all.

Ignoring the glass beneath her bare feet, Kate rushed to the broken window and leaned out into the dying light. Holding her breath. Listening.

Lifting one hand and waving when she heard it.

There.

Above the perpetual background noise of the city, the soft flutter of wings.

ORDER FORM

Fax your order to 303-694-4098 or
Mail to: StarsEnd Creations
8547 East Arapahoe Road #J224
Greenwood Village, CO 80112

TITLE	AUTHOR	ISBN	PRICE	QTY
Shakespeare's Confession	Para	1-889120-02-2	$19.95	_____
She Died Young	Livingston	1-889120-04-9	$ 8.95	_____
CrackedWEB, The Book	Richardson	1-889120-03-3	$12.95	_____
The Star Dwarves Trilogy	Richardson	1-889120-06-5	$12.95	_____
Take A Number *Poetry In E-Motion*	Maybury	1-889120-08-1	$10.95	_____
Distinctly Delicious *Favorite Recipes of the Distinctive Inns of Colorado*	Dist. Inns	1-889120-07-3	$17.95	_____

SIGNED COPIES AVAILABLE UPON REQUEST

Make checks or money orders payable to: StarsEnd Creations

Date: _____ PO # _____

Ship to:

_____

_____

_____

Bill to (if different than above):

_____

_____

_____

Phone #: _____ Fax #: _____